Ostara In the Sky

Where possibilities are endless

Paige Mirco

A reconnection to limitless possibility through a remembering of the magic that is available within the imagination.

Dear Chelsea,
May your heart always
lead the way & your
dreams come true!
♡ Paige +

To my Dad for being my greatest teacher and encouraging the divine curiosity within me.

To my best friend Ellie for encouraging the light of the writer in me to shine into the world

To my muse for inspiring the words spilled across these pages.

Lastly, thank you, dear reader, for being here and receiving your own flavour of magic.

Introduction

Imagination is the gateway to the expression of our heart's desire, the truth of human existence. It is the art form of the human mind that leaves behind one question...

What if?

One question that opens doors to more, to something greater, to possibilities that may not have felt available before.

So often, we use the magic within our imagination to avoid painful outcomes, or to try and fix or predict that which we would not love.

What if we utilised our imagination to dream a new world into being knowing that we are both the dreamer and the dreamed at the same time?

What if... anything is possible if we can imagine it?

What if... you can, if you imagine that you can?

What if... healing was one imaginative thought away?

What if... is a question that leads to more.

The question of what if led me down a path that was created by the opportunities that arose from the question.

I found wonder in the worlds of the pain I felt that led me to an adventure through my darkness with curiosity to understand the point of its existence. I felt wonder in the world of deep emotion that I experienced and what information lays within it. I felt wonder in the worlds that exist within worlds and I dedicated a life to exploring those worlds, not to separate from this world but to be more in this world. I allowed the wonders of the what ifs to take me to what's possible, to bring back the magic of dreaming into a world that has fallen asleep to the dream.

So to does your innocent heart know what is possible.

Children are so easy to love because of their innocence. They find magic in the mundane of inanimate objects and bring to life the personalities that they see within those objects. Their innocence has not yet been tainted by the illusion of the limitations that adult minds subscribe to.

Our hearts are innocent like children, it knows no limitations, only possibility, curiosity and wonder.

Vivid memories of my childhood are etched in my mind of starring at the stars in the clear skies of my home amongst the trees. I would stare and wonder who was out there? What was out there? And wishing they will come and visit us. I would dream of the day that interdimensional beings would come to visit me and show me magic tricks.

One day, they did but in a way that I wasn't expecting. They came to me through my imagination during deep meditation and found a home within my consciousness becoming my greatest allies and teachers.

My heart new more life forms were possible and my curiosity of the possibilities lead to a more magical and connected life.

Imagination is what makes life possible, and creation is what makes life tangible. We all have a limitlessness within us that is begging to be discovered.

It all starts to unfold with a simple question...

What if?

Here within this book, I am guiding you into the art of healing through your imagination. Here I am to deliver you the gift of remembering the joy that lies in dreaming all your truest possibilities into existence. I am here to remind you of feeling emotions, feeling your connection to everything through all time and space so you can allow the magic to unfold.

There is nothing braver and more courageous than choosing love in each moment and what love is, is an integration of all expressions of self which also encompasses all external to self.

To the depth of which we see, feel and know our darkest of self is the depth of love that we conjure.

What if... There is more to love? Even if it's in the dark. Can we shine a light on what we cannot see so we can see more? This has been my journey in life.

Some have called me crazy; some have loved me to death, some have witnessed my darkness and some only come to play in my lightness.

Yet as long as my heart is always beating, I will always have love to come home to and so do you.

Because love is woven through it all if we choose to see it.

My hope with this book is that you find inspiration in your internal world, the world and other worlds, to bring back more of you that was destined to be found in a world searching for itself.

May your heart always lead the way.

Love Paige,
An ever unfolding heart.

Chapter One

I am Dad

"She's here! She's coming, this is it!" Ange yells with a squeal of delight. A meadow of flowers rolling over the hills and over the horizon; a sunset that only magic could create. What a glorious sight that we behold. What a magical experience I have as a memory to tell my new daughter. I wish I could take a photo of my emotions so I can hold this feeling forever.

I look over to my wife who is crouched on all fours, glowing with pain and pride at the same time as she pants through the contractions. I feel an overwhelming sensation in my body, I am not familiar with this feeling, this feeling of love. It is like an expansion in my chest, and an openness in my breathing, it's like the warmth of the sun but it radiates internally. It's a feeling that isn't taught, it is mostly to be pushed aside, as love is for fairies. Fairies. I used to believe in fairies, I used to think that I saw fairies, but I must have been imagining it as a child. Children do that. The imaginary thing. Speaking of children, I am about to have one. My first, and I think she is a girl, I don't know how I know but I just know. Father instinct I guess.

Ok Carl, snap out of this daydream, this out of body love experience, back to reality where you need to do your job as a man. Be a man. Support your wife.

"ARRGGHHHHHH!"

Shit I'm not ready for this. Yes you are. You were born for this. You were born ready. Yup, I've got this.

"I can see her shoulders wiggling Ange, one more push, you've got this."

One more push from my warrior woman and the baby falls into my arms all gooey and blue. Kind of alien looking; yet a beauty I have never witnessed in all my years. A beauty that is indescribable. A wave of emotion comes over me and hits like a tonne of bricks, to my face, my stomach and my gonads. It feels like fire and water at the same time. It feels like immense pressure and ease at the same time. Weird yet so natural.

Somehow it feels like I am in a time warp, like time has stopped or sped up so fast that I don't know what is real. I look at my new daughter with eyes of wonder and she lets out a cry that echoes through the trees. She is here. She is *really* here. And Ange; what a soldier.

I wrap an old sheet around my new daughter to keep her warm and hold her to my heart. I am not really thinking at this moment, it is all instincts that are taking over.

Ange is laying on her back now, I assumed she was having a rest after such a long and hard labour, yet something doesn't feel right.

"Carl, can you hold me up so I can hold her?"

"Yes of course my love."

I gently use my free arm to elevate Ange's shoulders off the earth and take a seat behind her to hold her up, placing our child in the arms of her mother.

I feel the breath of Ange deepen as she touches our child; I follow and match so we can become in sync as a new family.

"She's perfect Carl, I am so in love," Ange says with exhaustion in her voice.

"She is everything we have ever dreamed and more, you have done well my love, I am so proud," I reply.

"She'll need you when she cries, she'll need you when she laughs, she will need you to remind her when she has forgotten the love in her heart. She'll need you when she is a babe and she'll need you until she tells you she doesn't, and even then, she will still need you. Carl, remember to support her in her emotions so she always remembers they are to be felt in their entirety. All so she can love as deeply as she hurts and so she can experience all that it means to be human. She'll be needing the direction of the masculine to support her in her feminine. And always remember the feminine within you. It is in the dance of the unity that this world needs and it is our duty to serve as the world as served us."

My breathing quickens and my heart starts racing. Anxiety kicks in. No no no no no no.

"Ange what do you mean I will need to, we're doing this together, it's *we* not I."

I feel her body starting to relax and our baby starts to cry louder. No no no no no.

"I am bleeding too much Carl. I'm not going to make it. I can feel it in my heart. We chose this paddock for the birth of our star child, we chose it all and I choose to leave this earth. It's a knowing; and now I am closer to the other side, I can feel the truth of choice. Promise me you will keep her safe and teach her to always choose from her heart."

"No no no no no no, Ange no, I promise all of those things but I also promised you my heart forever and to keep you safe." There is panic in my voice and daggers in my chest.

"Ostara, Ostara is her name. Be brave my love, have the will to always choose your heart, I love you."

This can't be happening, this, no. I can't - but we were meant to - I don't understand. Fuck.

Ostara is hysterical now and so am I. Tears fall from my eyes and cries rip from my mouth. I don't know what to do with myself. I touch Ange's face with my hand and keep the other hand on Ostara.

I look Ange in the eyes and she looks at me with deep love and joy, yet deep sadness. So beautiful even in a moment like this.

The trees around us start to whirl in the winds, and the grass we are laying in starts to dance around us. Ange takes a deep breath and sighs for what feels like a lifetime.

Time has stopped and it feels like my heart has too.

Daggers, more daggers in my heart. I crumble in pain. The breath I was praying Ange would take, never comes.

Chapter Two

Two days later – Carl

Pain. Intense pain wracks my body. Such intensity that I cannot fathom what reality is, what life is. I cannot comprehend or accept what has happened in my reality. What is reality? What is life? If there is a God out there, how can he/she possibly want me to go through something like this? I feel alone, I feel daggers in my chest, I feel disbelief in my mind and nauseousness in my stomach. Pain. Such pain.

Ange is not here. She is not here raising Ostara with me. I am alone in our humble home in the mountains. Alone. Shit. I am alone. Alone in this parenthood. We aren't meant to be alone in parenthood, we are meant to be doing it together. Isn't that what they say? It takes a tribe to raise a child. I am just a man, a man that doesn't reside in the mother instinct.

Numb. I feel numb, yet I feel so much all at the same time. I don't know how that is possible. Two days ago Ange was giving birth to our daughter and now she is gone, I had to bury my wife with a baby in my arms. A baby I haven't even been able to connect with yet. My capacity for feeling has been taken up by dread and pain, I want to feel connected to my daughter, but I don't know how yet. I don't know how to feel more than I already am. I feel numb to her, I feel numb to my newborn child, this is not how I had planned life. This is not how I imagined fatherhood.

Two days of trying to keep this child alive, while also trying to keep myself alive.

I look into Ostara's eyes and I see Ange looking back. I remember her words.

"Carl, remember to support her in her emotions so she always remembers they are to be felt in their entirety."

I feel the truth in the words she spoke but I have no idea how to support my daughter in her emotions right now, when all I feel is resentment. Resentment towards the world for taking my wife, resentment towards Ange for choosing to leave me, resentment towards Ostara for taking Ange's life, resentment towards myself for failing as a husband and a father. All I feel is burning flames in the pit of my stomach and daggers in my heart. As if someone has driven a knife right between my shoulder blades and twisted it in all directions. I haven't slept for two days; I can't stomach food because everything tastes like acid in my mouth. It baffles me that being human is the most painful thing of all time, it baffles me that we are to feel such immense pain, if God really existed then this wouldn't need to be. If love was all there is, then this shouldn't be happening. Pain shouldn't need to exist if love was all there was. That means love must not even be real, perhaps it's all a fantasy, perhaps it's just a story our parents tell us as children so we can feel better about living. Perhaps it's all a lie. Perhaps we are just here to be born, live, experience pain, sometimes experience happiness and then die to be food for the worms.

Ange was always a connected woman. She would talk to the trees, ask permission to pick any flower or leaf before she did. She would walk with such grace as though the wind was guiding her every step. She would speak to animals through her mind, or at least that's what she told me. I admired her in every moment we spent together. She was connected to everything, so connected to people around her, so connected to her body and sense of self. She always told me stories of her experiences in journeying into the cosmic realm and I always questioned whether she was crazy, but for some reason I never felt truth in her being crazy. I felt truth in her being connected. I never experienced what she did. I experienced it all through her by what she would tell me. I have always thought there was more out there than just this life on earth but now... now Ange has been taken away I can't connect to anything outside of this pain, not even my own daughter who Ange carried for nine months and who I would speak to through the womb. I can't see any way out of this pain.

Ange always told me that in order to really connect to your surroundings you had to feel. Feel your emotions, feel your surroundings, feel the sensations that would flow through your body in response to your surroundings. I always did my best to try and learn what she meant but I never fully grasped the concept of it. To me that was ok as just being with her was enough.

And now she is gone, now she has left this earth and I am here with Ostara, our child who I cannot connect with. The pain of that realisation causes another dagger to be driven into my heart. Why not have one from every direction? Why not just kill me now?

I wish Ange and I could switch places. She had so much greatness to deliver to the world and I am here completely... broken.

Ostara starts to stir from her sleep, gurgling and moaning as she brings her fresh tiny hands up to her tiny face. She lets out a little cry. I guess it's a cry for attention, but I am not one-hundred percent sure. Attention is all babies want right? I pick her up and tell her it is all going to be ok. What a lie.

As I hold her in my arms, I hear Ange's voice.

"She will be needing the direction of the masculine to support her in her feminine."

I hear her voice as clear as day, as though she is in the room with me, but it is in my mind. That doesn't even make sense to my brain, but I heard it and could feel her presence here. It feels so strange but so comforting at the same time.

I take some time to let the words sink in to my empty bottomless pit of a heart. She needs my direction, I must make a choice, I can't stay like this forever. In that moment I declare to always be the masculine in Ostara's life. There is only one kind of masculine I have ever known which came from my own father who was a war veteran. All I can do is do what I know. I choose to dedicate my life to her, to totally give her my life and never let her see my emotions. I choose to set my emotions aside to bring her into the world. In this moment I choose to man up and be the man this child can lean on. I choose to be a rock. Heart and all.

As I spell out these words in my mind the world around me starts to haze a little and all the sensations and feelings slowly dim and disappear as my heart closes tightly.

Chapter Three

The meeting

Thud, thud, thud. The sound of my feet as I run, run, run, heaving at the pace of my heartbeat but without a moment of thought to stop. I must keep running. I can't stop because he is chasing me. Billie is behind me and I cannot let him catch me. My ears burn from all the blood pumping in my brain and my chest hurts from the cold air pouring down my throat as I gasp for something more to keep my legs going. Never give up. Never surrender.

"Haya!" I scream out as I jump as hard as I can over a moss filled rock. I roll like an army soldier, hitting the ground as one of my legs gives way. Boy, I am good. I didn't even try to do that and it just happened. I'm a Ninja. Hot on my tail is Billie and I can hear him heaving but it is getting further and further away as I run. I don't look back. I must make it back to camp before he does. I will not surrender. I must win this. Not because it is life or death, but because I have to prove I am better… somehow. Like I am stronger than the boys. I will be stronger than the boys because if I am not then that means I am weak and I can't be weak. No way. Not me. Not Ostara. Not—

"Ahhh shit!" I scream as I kick the smallest of roots underneath a blanket of leaves on the earth floor.

I trip and I stumble as the inertia takes total control of my body. I can't save this. I am going over. Fuck.

I hit the dirt hard. My shoulder fails me as I tumble this time. My wicked army roll has failed me. I have failed me.

I feel no pain in my body, yet feel it somewhat in my brain. My body takes a while to catch up with the rest of my nervous system, finally moving quickly into position to let me know, that yes, I have hurt myself.

The movement stops and everything becomes still. I am heaving. Defeated. I lost. I am done. It all hits me. Fuck that hurts. There is a shooting pain from my ankle up the left side of my body and into my heart. But my ankle. Oh, my ankle hurts more than anything else. I think I have broken it or something. Surely the pain would be worse if I have broken it? I can't help but focus on the fact that I failed though. I failed the mission to beat Billie back to camp.

Oh yeah, Billie. I open my eyes to see him heaving over the top of me.

"Star, are you ok? That looked hectic! You hit the ground so hard and disappeared behind the tree so fast, it was almost like magic mate!" He squeals with excitement.

I sigh with annoyance. One big loud sigh.

"Yeah, I feel like I've broken something, have I broken something? I don't want to move right now, my ankle and left leg hurts so much," I say through pants of breath.

"Hmm… lemme check," says Billie.

He pats me down like a security guard checking for weapons.

"Oooh! Oh. Um. Ewww," he says.

My heart skips a beat. "Don't say it like that Billie! What's wrong?"

Before he can reply I sit straight up. I see Billie's face hovering over my ankle, staring, his face screwed up in confusion and disgust. Bending forward I wince through the pain to get a closer look at my ankle. Oh! I think to myself. My mind doesn't have room for any in depth thoughts, simply observation and emptiness. Shock. I think this is shock.

Blood is oozing from just above my ankle bone. No bones are sticking out, just blood oozing onto the earth floor. That is not the most shocking part though. What is shocking is that the blood oozing out is purple. It's not red. It is not normal blood colour and I can't understand it. The pain is still there but the shock has dissolved it into the background ever so slightly.

"Why is your blood purple? Did you eat too many beetroots?" Billie asks.

The humour of what he said made me giggle as it snapped me out of my shock which made me feel slightly better for a moment. Billie looked at me with a tight smile but the concern was still in his eyes.

"I don't know Billie. I really don't know."

We both get closer to my ankle, staring in curiosity. My blood is moving. Not in a normal blood way, oozing, trickling or pumping. It's moving in a way that is… not human. It is moving in a bubbling motion and as it hits the earth floor it disappears like there is no trace of the gory mess I am in right now.

In a protective, panicked sort of a way Billie takes off his shirt and wraps up my ankle to wipe away the visuals of something we have never seen before. Something so unknown.

"Are you ok though?" he asks again with concern in his voice as he brings his focus to my eyes now.

15

"I'm ok, I think I'm ok. The pain has lessened and I'm more curious now than anything else," I say.

With determination and curiosity to uncover my new-found purple blood, I gently push Billie's shirt down to see the broken skin.

"Sorry I just can't… I just need a minute," says Billie as he stands up, closes his eyes and turns around. He needs time to process what he just saw. I can read him so well. It is like he is trying to forget what he saw or trying to find some scientific explanation for it. Something like too many beetroots. I internally chuckle at him.

I bring laser focus to my ankle in fascination. As I gently wipe the blood away from the broken skin, what I see isn't a bone or peeled skin, but a marking in the shape of three triangles overlapping and a circle in the middle. I look around on the ground near me to see what kind of stick or rock could make such a symmetrical pattern on my skin. Nothing.

I look back at my leg in fascination. As my blood is bubbling with the tiniest of bubbles, the more I stare at it the more it slows and then the blood clots. This symbol is starting to heal at ridiculous speeds in front of my eyes.

Billie is still having a teenage crisis next to me. I can almost hear his internal thoughts.

Cool, I think to myself. I should feel scared right now but I don't. It somehow feels natural to me to see something so strange. The benefit of an open mind, I guess.

Out of the corner of my eye I see a green mist, or light, or something and my head snaps round. I watch the green mist gracefully floating through the bamboo forest and what looks like a holographic being, dressed in a black and gold cloak, forms in front of my eyes. I stare at the thing in wonder. The being raises… a what… a hand I suppose, to its mouth. Is that a mouth? Then it raises its finger in front of its mouth like it is shooshing me to be quiet. Gold and green dancing in and around the cloak.

"Shhhhhhh," penetrates through the forest and I feel the energy like a vortex through the trees. Then the being disappears. The shoosh radiates through my body and for some reason I still don't feel scared, just confused and in wonder at the same time.

The energy vortex through the trees creates a rustle that startles Billie out of his teenage crisis and I snap out of my trance and quickly cover my ankle. I didn't even think about it. It was like an instinct to protect him and me from whatever just happened.

"What was that noise? That was creepy. I think we should go. Can I help you to your feet or should I go and get someone?" Billie asks.

"No, I'm ok. I just need a hand up and I can walk," I say.

"Alright cool. I've got you," Billie says, as he pulls me up off the floor and throws my arm around his shoulder to help me walk.

"I know you do, you always do," I say with a slight smile on my face.

"Let's get you back to camp," Billie says with a calmer tone.

I stumble but I get my mobility back into my body and I look back to where the being was with more curiosity. I will think about this later. For now, Camp.

Eight-year old Ostara

Eight years earlier

"Daddy, Daaaaaaad, DADDY!"

"Oh, sorry love I am listening, I just went somewhere else for a moment," he said.

I pass him the candle that I have in my hand. "Now I want you to connect to the stars and make up a spell, in your own mind and speak it out loud," I instruct.

"I don't really know how to do that love. I'm not connected like that. Not like your mother was," he says with sorrow in his eyes and a wince in his chest.

"You can make a spell Daddy, or just make a wish, you can wish for anything. Magic is real and it will hear you. Maiden told me so and she isn't my imaginary friend, she's real. You just haven't noticed her yet," I say.

Dad chuckles and his belly bounces as he does. His belly of emotional heartbreak and the 'letting myself go because I can't care about myself anymore' kind of energy. It does make more of him to love though.

"You are so much like your mother Ostara, so much so. But I don't wish for anything, I don't wish for anything other than to be right here where I am with you," he replies.

"Everyone has something to wish for Daddy. If you don't want to make a wish then make up a magic spell. Maiden said that today was the day, that all the stars have aligned and that it's a special day to make commitments to aligning with our true stars," I plead. "I know you don't see her but she's real and I have to do what she says because… I don't know, it just feels right."

"Ok Ostara, ok." Carl, clears his throat.

"Almighty grace of light and dark,
Give me somewhat of a spark,
Share your knowledge on how to enter
and give space to what we call our centre
I am lost in all of this confusion,
Yet I know as she said, it's all an illusion,
Almighty grace let us share this time,
Together, so I can tell myself it will always be fine"

"Ok now light the candle," I tell him.

It is strange this feeling that I have. I don't know what it is but the only way I can describe it is a heaviness in my body. I feel a heaviness as I watch Dad light his candle. I look into his eyes and feel as though he doesn't see me; he doesn't feel me. I am desperate for his love and affection and to prove that I am good enough to be his daughter. See me Dad. I see you. He has never made me feel as though I am not loved, he has always told me, but I don't know why or how I know, but I don't believe it when he says it. I don't believe that he truly does love me. I am only eight-years old, I have been counting every birthday. I am eight-years and eighty-eight-days to be exact but I often feel like I am older than my dad. It is weird to think because I can't possibly be older than my dad because, well, he's old.

I have memories of everything, I remember everything from the moment I was conceived to the moment I was born in a paddock of bright green grass and flowers. I remember it all. I remember when I first saw Dad's face, the smell of him, like fresh rain in a forest. And my mum. I remember her pain as she pushed me out of her belly, I remember the feeling of her skin against mine and the knowledge in her eyes when she was saying goodbye.

It's weird though, I still don't feel like she is gone. I feel her around all the time and I hear her voice sing to me as I am falling asleep. She sings me lullabies and strokes my forehead.

But Dad has never been the same from what I remember in the womb. He would talk to me when I was in mum's belly. He would tell me that he will teach me all he knows about the world, how the cows make milk that can be turned into cheese, how the people of this town are crazy and wild but have good hearts. He said he would teach me how to have strong boundaries and never let them be crossed so I can always have my back, he told me he would love me until the ends of the earth and I believed him. That's the last time I remember believing him, eight-years and eighty-eight-days ago. I remember the moment he turned it all off. The light I felt in his heart flickered and went out. It stopped like a candle does when you blow it out on your birthday.

He doesn't know that I know, he doesn't know that I can feel as much as I do and a part of me likes it that way because he would never understand. He turned it off. I often feel as though I am old, much older than what I am. Often I feel as though I am the parent. The thoughts that run through my head are not of this world, they almost feel too much to be human.

When mum left this earth, I somehow knew that it was my duty to spread her message, her message of trusting in the thread that connects us all to one another. I heard her telling Dad how we needn't worry about what is coming next other than to take the next step from our hearts. As a baby I could always feel what mum was feeling and I never remember her feeling distress for longer than ninety seconds. I would feel this wave come over her and myself and it would move on within moments, it felt like a ride for me, like a dark impulsive wave would wash over me and it would scare me but excite me all at the same time. I remember mum feeling the same.

Remembering all of this makes me feel out of this world sometimes because I look at my dad whose light has completely dimmed in the heaviness of his own victim mentality. He is heavy and self-centred in his own pain. I feel his pain, yet I don't feel attached to it or him. Somehow, I know that he is my heaviest weight and my deepest challenge that I have chosen in this life.

"What do you want me to do now, love?" he asks.
I smile a slight smile, poor dad he has no idea.

"Close your eyes and imagine having all you've ever needed and wanted. Imagine you are already living everything you have ever desired and I will do the same."

I reach over and put a hand on his heart.

"And feel this."

I feel him contract and pull away from me like what I said has repulsed him.

"Or at least try and feel me," I say.

He opens his eyes, pain riddled through them, in disbelief of what I have said.

"You, my love, are just like your mother, you remind me of her every single day. You my love are wise beyond your years and it brings me pride and absolutely terrifies me at the same time," he says as his voice cracks.

He cups my face. His hands are hard from working too much and cold from his laziness to light the fire, I almost pull away from him at how cold they are but I stay so he knows I am listening. I see a golden thread that is coming from his heart that connects to mine, it looks like a small wire that would connect two lights.

It is a connection that I hadn't felt in a very long time.

"You Ostara will change the world through your very being. I don't know how but there is something truly special in you. You deserve so much more than me as a father but I will always do my best to love you as deeply as I can. You Ostara will show the word how to love again because you sure as hell couldn't be who you are and have me as a father if you didn't have that gift," he says.

He closes his eyes and takes a breath, a slow and shallow breath, as usual.

"Thanks Dad. I hope so," I say as he places his hand on my shoulder and gives it a squeeze. He smiles as I look up at him from the floor in front of him.

I see Maiden float in behind him now. To Dad, Maiden is my imaginary friend. She is child's play and I guess she is to some degree because I am just an eight-year and eighty-eight-day old child. Maiden is beautiful, she isn't human like at all. She wears a golden and black cloak. The inside is black and the outside has gold vintage patterns that connect in ways that could be a language, like there is a golden alphabet on her back. She is translucent and has no face but she is made of golden particles that form and reform into different expressions. She is like a shapeshifter but made from golden dust particles. We spend a lot of time together and we have for as long as I can remember. She was there when my mum died and she has been around ever since. She doesn't always speak or answer my questions but she sure as hell is bossy when she wants to be. I don't mind though. It's kind of nice having someone direct me when my dad is so absent. She teaches me things. A lot of things. Magical things. I guess it is because of her that I am 'so wise' for my eight-years and eighty-eight-days. I love her and I feel safe and nurtured by her in ways that most humans couldn't. I can't explain it and I don't feel like I need to because she is here for ME.

Maiden gestures with her ethereal particle hand for me to take her hand. So, I do. As I take her hand, she speaks to me telepathically in the most soft and gentle voice.

"Sweet child, you must forget me for some time. I cannot tell you why this is so but it must be," she says.

Sadness and confusion come over my body. "No. I don't want to forget you. If I forget you, then I will forget all the magical things we do and have done together. I will forget the best parts of my life. No. Why would you do that? Don't abandon me. Please don't," I plead in my mind as my eyes wince and a tear escapes me.

"Remember I told you that today is when the stars align. It is a special day. It is in your highest good to forget me today. One day you will understand. One day we will meet again but for today all you need to know is I love you and you will be safe. Trust in your heart always."

The words ricochet through my mind. She can't be serious. She said she would never leave. She said she would always be my friend. She said—

A lightning shock floods my body and I jolt awake. Was I asleep just then? Oh, nope me and Dad just did a candle thing that's right. I don't even know why we did that. I can't even remember what the point of it was. Huh. Weird. I feel confused.

"I think it is your bedtime missy. Let's go, this day has been long enough," says Dad.

I nod in respect to his instructions, feeling confused and slightly off but I respond by making movements towards bed.

Chapter Five

Year 12

The bell rings and it is time for lunch at Winshire High School. This is where I have the time to live some kind of normality. I have a few friends here, all whom I would choose over and over in every lifetime. School is the place where I can really put my head down into learning. I love science. I love it a lot. It feels so celestial for me, using it to figure out what all the amazing things of the world do and why. I still have no idea what I want to do in the world as a job but I know that I want to do something that will create a wave of change.

When I look around the corridors of the school, I see so many faces that are confused and uncertain about everything in their life, it is like they are floating through time and space without any direction. Like a bubble in the wind. Like they are in a dream. We ARE in a dream. A waking dream. It saddens me but then I also remember that I am one of those bubbles. It saddens me to be saddened by my own unknowingness and confusion. I wonder to myself everyday if there is something more, something greater, far beyond what we can possibly dream of and we all KNOW that there is because we can feel the truth in it but we just don't know how to get there. The magic and wonder have been lost from the eyes of the people who believe that this waking dream is nothing but tangible nothingness. I feel it all, I feel everything around me, all the people around me, the energy around me and in every moment I am breathing I feel like I am dying and living at the same time. Life is a paradox that I still haven't quite figured out.

I have friends here who I find joy in, who I love, but there is something deep inside me telling me there is something more. I wonder, I daydream every day. Is it possible to daydream in a waking dream?

I think about it all the time. We go to sleep. We dream. We wake up and dream again. What if we were wrong and our dreams were real and life was actually the dream. Trippy I know but I wonder. I wonder what's possible.

This is never taught in schools, that's the one thing that I wish schools would teach us. I wish school could be mysterious, like *Harry Potter's* Hogwarts. I am sure that's where I belong, casting magic spells, opening portals and dreaming in other dimensions. Surely that's everyone's destiny, to be more wondrous, or maybe I am judgemental of the mediocrity of this life.

Ok Ostara, I know we love to dream big and all but look around you, you are surrounded by people who don't understand, they don't care, they don't want to care. They are happy in their little lives, in their bubbles. Who are you to make a difference?

Ok brain, thanks for the input, can you be quiet now?

Um nope, you are just a human, do you really think that you can change people's lives? Pffft don't be daft. You can't change your dad's life so why do you think you could change anyone else's?

Ouch. I wince. That one hurt, brain. Fuck. I guess you have a point.

Just go about your day, Ostara and learn what you need to learn, get the grades, get the job, do the do, like you are meant to, and you will be fine in the world. Go with what is known, that's always the safest option.

I don't want to just be fine though. I want to live in joy, live in love, in somewhat of a feeling world. Where people feel things in depth and do things from love for love, not just for the sake of doing. Is that crazy or is that just connected? I would love to think it's connected. Can you get on board with that?

No, and yes, it is crazy, Ostara, the world is set here, the world is as it is. Just look at how it is and be in how it is. Change creates waves of attention. Do you really want all that attention on you?

Ok you have a point, brain. The thought of everyone staring at my naked soul, bared in my desperation for something bigger than all of this, freaks out my nervous system. Ok, let's focus on something else, let's focus on—

"Ostara!" I hear Billie bellow at me from down the hall. Speaking of creating waves of attention.

"Oh Billie," I say with a half giggle. "You startled me for a second."

"Are you ok? You look confused?

"I am ok man I was just deep in thought about something."

"As per usual," Billie replies with a smirk.

Billie is my oldest and craziest of friends. He has always lived a few kilometres down the road from our farm so we grew up together.

After my mum died the whole town pitied my dad for the loss and they would come over with cooked meals, clothes for me and always be willing to lend a hand. Of course, Dad never wanted to admit how much he was struggling. Since I was eight-years old, all I recall is wanting to leave the house and to be outside, to experience being a child and Billie was always ready to play. Margaret, his mum, would welcome me into their home and give me the warmest of hugs, the way only a mother could. It is something that I relished because I never had any from my own, not that I remember anyway. Billie and I have always had such fun together, he is a kind soul, someone who takes the time to listen and care for you in a time of need. Although I never admit that I need him because I like to be independent. I guess I always have been. I'm the adult so I have never needed help, or so I tell myself. It is easier that way.

As friends we have got up to some crazy things that were NEVER my idea, always Billie's. He would insist that I run and try back flip into dams, ride push bikes off jumps, build cubby houses that were severely unstable (a bit like my father) and insist I trust him in their building. Of course, every time I would trust him it would turn into a disaster but I never regretted a second of it because he always made me laugh, even in the most frustrating of times. He is like a breath of fresh air.

"Hey, I wanted to ask you how your ankle is going after camp? Has it healed?" Billie asks. Always so caring. He never forgets to check in, ever.

"Oh, I completely forgot about that. It's completely fine. I have a scar there now, it's just a light scar though, like a tiny very sharp pen drew on me," I say as I lift up my daggy school pants.

"It's kind of… art. It doesn't look like a scar. It looks like someone *actually* drew on you. It looks like a symbol from one of those really weird Viking pagan times. Are you sure you didn't draw that on yourself in one of those weird, dreamy states you go into?" he asks with a raised eyebrow. It's like he's interrogating me so he can understand the logic behind my scar.

I chuckle but am a little annoyed by his statement that my dream states are weird.

"First of all, they aren't dream states, they are real states and second of all, if you would remember correctly, you were there when I tripped over. Do you think I had the time to whip out a knife or pen and carve a symbol into my ankle? AND didn't you also see me bleeding from that same place? Purple blood if you remember," I say with fire in my voice.

Billie's shoulders roll in and his stomach contracts like his internal organs had a seizure. He does not like the memory of that day at all.

"Yeah, I remember, you ate too many beetroots and were bleeding purple," he says sharply. He doesn't want to go there or think about it.

I accept this, yet I know it is more. I always know there is more, but he doesn't want to know, even though he does know. I get it and I love him regardless.

"Anyways, I'm all good now and it has healed and I think my scar is pretty bad ass don't you?" I say with a smirk.

"Yeah, you will always be badass Star. You're one of a kind. One that I don't always understand, but one that is cool as fuck" Billie says, throwing his arm around my neck in joy and pulling me in the direction of our next classroom.

"Can I come over later? I'd love to talk to you about something, get your perspective on what you think I should do and I'd like to go to our magical paddock near the pine trees?" he asks.

Before he even finishes his sentence, I have a feeling. A niggle in my heart. I can't explain it, but I know he is going to ask me for girl advice about Melina. He has never said anything to me about her before, but I can see a kind of twinkle in his eye when she walks past and almost a skipping of his heartbeat as she doesn't notice him. I guess it has always been obvious to me. I have this weird way of knowing things and not knowing how or why I know them. Especially when it comes to people who I am connected to.

"Would this have anything to do with Melina in your maths class?" I ask directly.

I feel his body jolt slightly in awkwardness, like he just got caught out masturbating. Which I have no doubt he most definitely does.

His body settles quickly as he remembers he is safe with me and he bows his head shyly.

"I am such a twit when it comes to girls. Apart from you I don't know how to interact with other girls that I have a crush on. Like how do you even communicate? All I ever do is go awkward and scare them away and I am so certain I want to make an impression on this one, so I was thinking, if you can pretend to be me and I can pretend to be her you could talk to me like I should be talking and then I can learn, ya know?"

"Right. Ok. Hmmm. Well. Ummm," I sigh.

"And what better place to do it than at the magical field. Since we have always declared that space to be magic then I am sure it will work wonders on my wooing abilities, right?" His voice is hopeful.

I sigh a long sigh. "Life is never boring around you. Yeah sure, why not? Maybe it will work wonders on my relating too," I reply.

"Fuck yeah! You are the best Ostara. Thanks. Can we leave the rest until later? I don't want her to walk past and hear us?" Bille says.

I smile a hearty smile and give another sigh. Not of judgment but of love for his soft and vulnerable heart in this moment.

"Yes of course my friend. Of course, we can wait." I tug on his arm directing him towards our next class. "Let's get this last class over with and we can go and have a *deep and meaningful*. I've got you, don't you worry."

I have no idea what I will say to him in the field, but I am excited for the journey. Something feels different about today. I don't know why, but it feels like there is more to this conversation with Billie. Like the energy around me is palpable yet invisible. I don't know what it is yet, but it feels very similar to my experience running in the bush at camp. Like worlds are colliding and I am the centre point. The only one that can see, feel and know what is happening in other worlds yet at the same time the only one who other humans can see.

I wonder. My mind wanders, for a moment and I let it go.

"Hey," Billie says interrupting my thoughts. "What were you thinking about earlier? I don't know why but I feel the need to ask again. Something is telling me," he says, side eyeing me with curiosity as he makes a movement with his hand over his head as if to say that 'the something' is a woo woo thing that isn't real.

"You know, the same old Ostara stuff. Like what are we doing here. What else could be more than this. Thinking the big thoughts of possibility, ya know?" I reply.

"Oh yep, that's a 'you' thought. If we were to have something big happen, it's gotta be in the magical paddock because that's the most magic place to us, so if nothing has happened until now, I reckon having a gender swap role convo would do the trick." He crumples into a half bend in laughter. I glare in a mocking way at him but I can't help but giggle with him. He always knows not to take life too seriously. It's nice for such a deep thinker like me.

"Well, I guess we will find out tonight, I am open to it, if there is something," I say.

"And I read that it is a Scorpio full moon tonight too," he says.

"Since when did you start reading about astrology mate?" I ask in shock.

"I thought it might be a nice touch to add into my date with old girl when she decides she loves me. Chicks love that astrology shit, right?" he asks.

I face-palm. What a dude. "I've got to hand it to you, you're a real charm. I do have to agree though. Astrology is an in for most girls. At least I think it is. I'm not great with women but I know that I love astrology so I think most would be stoked with a bit of knowledge in that area. I had forgotten about the full moon tonight, but I knew something was up because my thoughts were even deeper than normal. Ya know, those kinds of thoughts you have when you are feeling like something strange is about to happen, not bad but unknown, ya know?"

"Only you would know, Ostara," Billie replies.

I smile at him and we keep making our way to the class.

Yeah. only me. Only the crazy thinker Ostara. The one who feels too much and thinks too deeply. The believer. The weirdo. The hearty helpless. Ostara. The one who killed her mother.

Chapter Six

Homecoming

It's time to go home. For some reason I feel a sense of relief that the end of school bell has rung and it is time to go home. Usually, I am writing like a mad woman taking down as many notes as possible because, hey I'm a nerd, but today feels different. I feel the need to head home and have some time in the paddock that Billie and I, for most of our lives, have declared to be magic. Today, it feels like something is in the air. I have never been able to communicate with words that well when I feel something. I feel, see and know things but it is hard to explain it to other people, so usually I don't. I keep it to myself. Today is one of those days when I feel, see and know something is in the air but can't explain it. This isn't like any normal day.

We are all hustling to get out of the classroom and it is me who is first to the door. Strange again. Usually I am the last. Mr Miller even gives me the side eye as if to say, 'Are you ok Ostara'. Oh, I'm totally fine Mr Miller, just rushing home to perhaps cross-dress with my friend, don't mind me! I think, but don't say. Instead, I give him an awkward smile and leave quickly.

I meet Billie in a corridor that smells like old cheese and teenage sweat and we journey home, taking our usual daily route through the tree forest. We could just as easily take the bus but it is always nice and refreshing to be outside. Argh nature, it does things to me. I can't tell you what it does but it's something and that's all I have to express it, again my words fail me. We pass the usual paddock of cows and we do our usual animal communication technique of mooing at them to see if they respond, and they do every time. Every time we do this it always feels like I can understand them. *Yep Ostara, you have officially lost it. Cows don't speak English. They don't communicate like we do. In fact, they are just cows, they eat grass and they are on autopilot. Their only purpose here is to be cows and only cows.*

Ok brain, calm your farm (no pun intended) just let me feel like there is something more for a second, ok?

Thinking there is something more is dangerous Ostara. Thinking that you can live with more grandeur on this earth is stupid, outrageous and no one will like you if you try to outlive them anyway.

Right. You are right. But just let me talk to cows and imagine that I can, thanks.

The noise in my mind goes silent and I sigh.

"Yo Billie, I reckon you've got a pretty good chance at taming the wild heart of Melina and sweeping her off her feet like Cinderella!" Billie says. I look at him, confused. "What?"

"That's what that cow said to me, he told me that. Its total confirmation that this therapy session will absolutely get me over the line," he says as he makes movements with his hand like he is throwing a fishing line into the water and reeling it in.

"You're fishing, well if that's the case then I will validate you to make you feel a little more confident. Whatever you put your mind to Billie, you can do it. You are the man, you've got this, you can achieve the stars and all the planets in the galaxy, you can bring heaven to earth just by being you." I fist pump for a few seconds after I have rambled a whole bunch of hype girl vibes at Billie and he stops in his tracks with a quizzical look on his face.

"Thanks, Ostara, I can always count on you to be my hype girl even if you are lying to make me feel better. It's weird, ya know, I always feel like you can see through my fears," he says.

"Well Billie, I have known you since we were tiny tots. It's not hard to read what you need. Oh! Fuck yeah! Did you hear that! I am a poet and I know it," I squeal with excitement and wink at Billie. He face-palms and giggles at the same time.

"You are one of a kind my friend. One of a kind," he says with a smirk.

After forty-five minutes of walking down the winding forest road, we arrive at the rusty old gate to the farm I call home. My home is so beautiful, it is old and rustic but it has such a feel of freedom. Like it has been abandoned and nature has taken over. It has a feeling to it, that if it could speak to you, it would say home is where the heart is, and home is amongst the trees. I don't know if you could call that a feeling but it makes sense to me. As you walk up to the old rusty gate, surrounding you are fields of grass, and just before the horizon, hills start to form and in the further distance you can see fields of flowers. Spring is in full bloom right now and it is my favourite time of year because all the babies are born, all the flowers bloom, more love and juice is squeezed out of life in the people around me, there is so much newness in the air. It's like the earth has its own rebirth and I love watching how the world wants to express itself after a time of symbolic death and hibernation through winter. As the afternoon creeps in over the hills and fields, the sun is warm and so golden that you can stare at it without hurting your eyes. I love doing this. Normally I will do it with my feet on the earth, it makes me feel connected to something greater than myself, like the sun is this giant hot light bulb in the sky. All I see is light, this ball of white light floating in the sky, radiating heat. How cool is that to think about. A floating ball of light. It sounds like something out of a magical children's book. It sounds crazy to most but I like to think magic is real and the sun is somewhat of a portal to somewhere more magical than here.

Billie and I are mucking around as we walk down my long and windy driveway. We're making up stories about the grand scheme of life, if we had magical powers to change the way the world was, what we would change and what we would do. We come up with all sorts of wild things, like magical trees that could speak to us, portals, giants, nymphs, talking cows and other animals, rainbows that you could slide down and land in a world of lollies and candy but the kind of candy that was good for you and when you ate it; it would make you fly. This is one of the things I love most about our friendship. Weird is normal and normal has no definition for us.

We come to the end of the driveway and walk up to my little cottage of a home. It is old, wooden, rustic and almost looks decrepit. Haunted yet homely, like the walls have a thousand stories to tell. Every day I walk up to my home I have a moment of appreciation for having a home. After all life is so very short as I always think of my mum when I see home, she is always here and her presence is tangible, like the viscosity of water around me. But today; it's different. I feel this slight tension in my gut, heaviness in my mind and a sense of nauseousness. Strange. *Come on, Ostara your whole life is strange, you really think this is strange? We are always anxious and feel like something is missing. What's new?*

Yeah, fair enough brain, let's be logical here. It's just a feeling. We are good. No stress. Nothing to see here at all.

"Hey kids," Dad says from the rocking chair on the front porch. He has a half empty glass of beer in his hand.

I startle out of my in-depth thoughts.

"Woar!" I take a deep breath in to let that rush of adrenaline flush through me like my breath is water. "Hey Dad, you startled me, what have you been up to today?" I ask.

"Hey Mr Gregory!" says Billie with a big grin on his tanned and defined face.

So formal. I think to myself. There is something in the air today.

"Hey Billie. I've been sitting here for quite some time. I cleared the sheds today and went through some old things of your mother's, Ostara. I left what I thought was of value on the back porch to either sell or give to you. I thought it was about time I did so. Something came over me today and I just decided that it was time and started getting to work," Dad says.

My heart sinks as I remember my mother's presence is still here. Will that mean that her presence will leave? Does that mean that her spirit won't live on anymore? Does she think that we don't love her if we get rid of her stuff? Maybe she will like that dad is moving on after sixteen years. Or maybe she will be able to cross over now that she doesn't have an attachment here. Wow so many thoughts, so much noise. I take a moment to take a deep breath. Dad is fragile. I always feel like I am walking on eggshells when it comes to talking about Mum so now that he has brought it up I feel even more uneasy, but the breath helps.

"Oh.. well that's great Dad, it's great you felt motivated to be doing that today. I want to go through it all before you take it anywhere," I say in a hurry as if I don't get the words out now they will never come out.

"Yes of course love. I wouldn't get rid of it before you go through it first," he says.

"Let's go, Billie, I want to look through this stuff before we head off to the magic spot this afternoon," I say.

I shuffle my feet like the life has been kicked out of me, or a heavy blanket has been thrown over me, and I must carry it like my life depended on it. Billie puts his hand on my shoulder without saying a word. He is intuitive like that; he knows when something heavy has got my heart. I tap his hand as if to say, 'thanks man but I am ok'. I don't like people fussing over my emotions. It's uncomfortable. It makes me want to crawl out of my skin.

Am I ok? Yup, I think I am ok, hold your chest high and take some deep breaths. We will be fine, it's just stuff, I think to myself as I try to escape my emotions.

We go through the back door. My heartbeat raises as I see a pile of things that has the essence of my mother all over it. Some would call me crazy because I was a newborn baby when my mother died so how could I remember anything of her, but I do, or maybe I am imagining that I do. I remember the feeling of her. Either way it is comforting.

"Woah, how cool!" Squeals Billie.

Really Billie. It is not the time to be in such excitement. At least one of us is excited right now.

"Look how cool this stuff is, Star. There's a goblet, some lit cards, you know those cards that tell your future and shit and there is some weird looking hippie drum, ooh and there are some clothes here. We could wear some of them tonight for a special occasion. If that's ok with you, or something you want to do?"

Boy. Instant overwhelm. It feels like there are so many questions at once. My heart feels like it is going to drop out of my chest and my mind is so full it feels like it has dropped onto the ground. I am shocked by her stuff being out. The feeling is surreal.

"Um… I… Um. Can I answer you when I have gone through it all first? I mean it should be ok but I want to see which bits I DON'T want you to grub up."

He smiles a gentle smile and nods in honour of my request as he places a hand on my shoulder. "Sorry I shouldn't have been so intense about it. This must be strange for you," he says as he lowers his head to meet my eye gaze.

I take a deep breath and nod. I have no words, so I start rummaging through the messy pile that my dad created. Geez you would think that he would have placed them nicely. Dad is a lost soul so he doesn't think of things like that.

My mother's smell still lingers on her clothes as I pick them up to inspect them. Her smell blends with a slight muskiness of oldness. This is wild. After sixteen years of being in the shed they should smell like mould and mouse poop but they still have her smell. Like lavender and honey. Her smell was calming and soothing and that is exactly the feeling that I get while going through her things.

Without even thinking I place the goblet and tarot cards aside in the keeping pile.

"Good choice," says Billie.

I pick up the first piece of clothing that is made of silk and bury my face into it, taking a deep breath in to fill my lungs with the love of her presence. I take another deep breath in just to be greedy in the calmness that it invokes in me. Memories, pictures, flash before my eyes and I know they are memories of her because it feels familiar yet I don't have any memory of her. In every memory she is smiling and I can feel the magic in her, it is the way she moves and smiles in such grace, it's how I can tell. I have a moment of wishing I was like her, wishing I could remember more of her, so she could guide me home to a place that only she knows. I sigh as I find more calmness in her scented presence.

I throw over a few pieces of clothing that I think Billie might love as he has always been a bit of an odd ball when it comes to fashion. Sharing my mother's clothes with him makes me feel lighter. Like it is not as big a deal than what I think and feel.

"Yahh, floral! Just my style!" He squeals and fist pumps like an old sailor. He quickly puts the floral dress over the top of his school uniform and asks, "How do I look?"

"Like a real twat," I reply with a smirk and await his comeback.

"But it will do the trick if you fancy it. If you feel happy in it, that's all that matters," I continue.

I continue rummaging through the clothes but am brought to a standstill. I feel a buzzing as I pick up a kimono jacket. Well at least I think it buzzes, but anything with a battery wouldn't have lasted this long in the shed. I search the jacket pockets where I felt the buzz come from and find a ring. It doesn't look like a wedding or engagement ring though, it's more like a ring full of rainbow stones. A rainbow ring.

"Cool, that's pretty. Can I wear that?" Billie jokes.

"No way," I reply sharply as Billie pulls his hand back from launching to grab it in his excitement.

"I'd like to wear this tonight. It feels really special as I've never worn any jewellery of Mum's. I didn't even know there was any. It's something we can use for good luck to get us through your training tonight," I say.

"Alright alright, fair enough. I think a dress and hat will be fine. I feel a little lavish to be honest, a bit right wing, an odd ball if you will and I kind like it," he responds.

I smile at Billie but I am distracted by the ring. It feels almost sacred, like I am only allowed to put it on at certain times. Special times. And by special I mean when I NEED it. I guess I will know when or I'll feel it.

"I reckon I'm finished with everything I want to keep, everything else will be a gift for someone else I guess. Some lucky person from the second hand shop who is in need of some of Mum's energy." I feel a pang in my heart as my body remembers that all of this won't be in the house, her energy won't be as loud here. A moment of grief dips into my chest but I shrug it off.

"Come one, let's go get all of your things off your chest," I say.

I smile a soft smile as I still feel a slight pang in my heart. Billie gently nudges me on the shoulder with a soft fist in a playful manner and we make our way back outside towards the magical paddock.

Chapter Seven

The Meeting

The ground is cold and muddy on my feet. Fresh rain has made the ground soft and it squishes between my toes. I love it when the ground is like this because I love the sensations of the earth on the nerves of my feet. It's like this sensation of pleasure shoots up my legs and into my pelvic area and every time it activates something in me, a desire. I am not sure what the desire is yet, but it feels animalistic, that's the best word I have to describe it.

We approach our arrival at the magical paddock. It is covered in stones, small ones, big ones, oddly shaped ones, as if the stones were individually handcrafted and placed there by giants. That's the first thing that comes to mind whenever I look at them and I like to imagine that giants are real sometimes, nice giants though, like the one from the Big Friendly Giant movie. The land oscillates in such a flow, like a green ocean that calmly moves with a gentle breeze. There are dips to walk through and small hills to climb, but each hill is not really a hill, yet it feels like an achievement every time we get to the top of one. Some of the stones are so large they have smaller ones sitting on top. It is strange to the eye as the stones on top are circular and I have always questioned why they haven't fallen off yet or been blown off by a storm. It baffles me every time as I try to work it out logically. So I don't.

In the distance I can see the field of flowers that I was born in and how each flower dances in the slight breeze. It is warm tonight; the clouds are thick yet sparse in the sky and the atmosphere has such a density that it almost feels sultry. Every step I take is like wading through warm water, as I walk, I dance my hands in and around myself to play with this strange density of the air.

Billie is up ahead, leading the way, a typical man wanting to show the woman the directions, yet he is dressed as a woman which makes me giggle at the irony of it. I am ok with it because I am in such a trance with this strange viscous energy around me, it's like I don't feel separate from anything and I haven't felt this before. It's strange but I kinda like it, it feels normal. My kind of normal. A weird normal.

I have my mother's ring in my pocket, I haven't been able to put it on even though I have wanted to but I have the feeling that I am going to need it tonight. I don't know how I know that but I do, perhaps to save me from myself in some way.

As we get closer to the largest stone in the whole paddock I start to feel palpitations in my chest, not the kind that means you need to go to hospital or anything, the kind that feels like a butterfly is sitting in the middle of my stomach and tickling the edges of my skin. I feel the density of the earth and air around me get a little heavier, like I am walking into a sleep.

"Hey Billie, can you feel that?" I ask.

"Feel what?"

"The…" I pause. "The heaviness? Like the air in an ocean of warmth and coziness or something of the sort?" I say.

"Um, no. Are you ok? Or have you just picked up some random flower, eaten it and gone to fairyland? I feel warmth but that's all. Oh, and relief for what is about to unfold," he says.

I feel as though there is more to what he is saying that he even knows. There is a high-pitched ringing in my ears when he says the words 'what is about to unfold' and my head cocks to one side as I am trying to understand the internal sensations.

I get nervous and a little anxious of the unknown but I keep moving at what seems like the slowest pace possible. One step in front of the other.

"In all seriousness though, Ostara, are you feeling ok?" Billie asks as he turns around to examine me.

I take a moment to register what he asks. Information is computing slower, but computing nonetheless. "Yeah, I'm ok, just a little dazed but I'm fine," I respond.

"Great because I'm feeling like we are really going to go somewhere. We always find directions with our chats that are unexpected," he beams.

Again. The words he speaks feels like it means more than he even thinks it means. Maybe I am going crazy, maybe I am in fairyland, maybe there is something wrong with me. I mean if I was special, like my mother said before she died, then maybe my dad wouldn't be so miserable all the time. He does his best to hide it from me but I have always known what is underneath.

"Buckle up princess," comes from a voice that didn't sound like Billie's. Or maybe it was and I am imagining things. I shrug it off and quiver as I repeat the sound of the voice in my head.

That was *definitely* not my own voice in my head, or Billie's voice, or anyone's voice I have ever heard before.

With every step I feel heavier in my body and have a ringing in my head. It is like someone is hitting one of those triangles I use in music class, but the sound of it is never ending.

Wet muddy feet, heavy hands in a sea of energy around me, a ringing in my head, a heaviness in my chest and a pulse running from the earth through my feet into my pelvis is my entire reality right now; it is all I feel, it is my entire experience yet I am somehow still aware of everything around me. My feet are still moving, albeit at the slowest pace I have ever seen in my life. I am looking down at them as I walk to take my steps with absolute caution.

"Woohoo we made it!" Billie squeals as he turns around to look at me.

"I would like to lay down and look at the sky while we chat, would you like to lay down too?" he continues.

I nod in agreement. Laying down is the only thing I want to do right now as my body is as heavy as I have ever felt. Like I have gained 100kg in the last thirty minutes, if that is even possible.

We lay down head-to-head as if we are sharing brain energy. My breathing is slowing and everything feels peaceful, so peaceful. Everything is worrying me and everything has me curious at the same time.

Everything is in slow motion now. Even Billie's voice as he starts to pour his heart out to me about Melina.

My breath is the loudest part of my existence and as I take the deepest breath in, it feels like my last. As I exhale I melt into the ground like a puddle of water.

There is a crash of thunder in my mind, my pocket sends a gentle electric shock through my nervous system and as I place my hand on top of my pocket to gain a sense of whether the electric shock was real, I slowly raise my head through the dense air around me and that air is sparkling blue. Prickles of blue dance in and all around me.

Buckle up princess, buckle up princess, buckle up princess is all I could process in my mind. What does that mean? What am I buckling up for? Curiosity sweeps through my heart and openness enters my mind as I slowly rest my head back down to the earth underneath me. I breathe out again. I melt even further into the earth and I close my heavy eyes and the earth caves in around me.

I am no longer in my body. No longer… human. I'm just… my mind. A consciousness floating through what feels like a wormhole, or portal, or a fun fair ride of my lifetime.

I land… somewhere. Someplace. It feels familiar but I can't quite see anything, only feel and see darkness.

I focus on what I do feel so I can orientate myself to what is happening. I feel uncomfortable, unsafe in some way. Fear. That's what it is. Uh Oh! I think to myself.

And then, I smell burning flesh mixed with a herb-like aroma, perhaps sage, but I can't quite pinpoint the herb over the stench of flesh, at least, I think it is flesh. My senses open more as I focus on the smell and what seems like a static sheath of darkness starts to dissipate, to show a vision behind it. I float through with my ethereal body.

I see a man, a shaman; the wolf skin on his head is a dead giveaway. His face has seen many lives come and go and each has created many lines. His eyes are deep and soulful, yet wicked in wisdom. His demeanour is powerful, unfuckwithable but nurturing at the same time. In his left hand he holds a staff which has a white selenite crystal nestled in the crest of it. We are in an open cave, seated around a fire. I start to realise more as the vision opens more, as I open myself to the detail.

"It is time," he says with a terrifying certainty to his voice.

Time for what? I think to myself.

"Time for your initiation," he says.

He just responded to my thoughts. He just did that. That just happened. I talk to myself to try and gather some understanding of this reality.

"I am your guide, a friend from past lifetimes that has a contract with you, to guide you through this particular initiation. We have met before, spent much time together, you simply don't recall it in human time. We met in the times of human sacrifice that rightfully no longer exists in your world. But it does in some worlds and you need to be initiated into your power now to help. You are a key. You won't understand right now, but you will," he says.

He points his crystal crested staff in the direction of the deep dark cave.

"You must go. Go through that cave and you will find the truth of your darkness which has held you back for many years. Be brave and hold strong, you cannot be harmed. Simply be in the experience. I will call you back to Billie when the initiation is complete," he says matter-of-factly.

"Before I go anywhere, I have a question. Where is my physical body? And what is happening to me?" I think to him.

"You are astral projecting, Ostara. Your body is still back on earth with Billie but your ethereal body is exploring your own internal yet external world through astral projection.

Astral projection has always been a gift of yours, you have simply forgotten for reasons you will soon find out," he says with a slight smile on his face. The first smile I have seen yet. "One last thing, when you need to, you may call upon your ally, Tanarous. Only when you need her. You will know." He speaks calmly now and smiles his second smile. Calmness sweeps through my ethereal body and without a second to ponder on who Tanarous is, I have entered the cave.

Chapter Eight

The Initiation

I feel a sense of popping out the other side of the darkest cave on earth. The opening has become apparent in my awareness but without seeing it through the darkness, just knowing and feeling it. I wait a moment, to see what will happen next. It's like a movie is happening in front of me and I am in the experience but not of it. I zoom in my focus as the dusty smoke of my confusion starts to open into a wonder again and what I see is terrifying, unpleasant in every sense of the world. Every particle of me wants to suck myself back to my shamanic guide, back to my human body, but the sun in my centre in holding me here, my innate power and I know deep within that I cannot leave. You cannot be harmed rings through my mind, the words of my guide. I cannot be harmed, I cannot be harmed, I repeat to myself. Focus here, Ostara, focus. I focus on what I can see. A child in chains, naked, bruised and beaten, sad and alone, bewildered and completely powerless. She is shackled to the dark ground, slumped forward on her knees, head in her hands. Hopeless. She looks to be about six-years old. She is so tiny. I feel my ethereal heart ache, if that is possible. I feel the emotion of grief and my natural reflex is to comfort her, I want to save her but I am confused as to how she is here and why this is happening to her, I am frozen in myself, unable to move.

49

I can't tell if anything is around her. All I can see is darkness. All I feel is heat. It is hot here. Incredibly hot. A loud voice echoes through this hot and dark space and it shocks me into presence.

"Hello Ostara, it is nice to finally meet you."

My ethereal throat tightens and my freeze response continues. I want to curl up and dissolve into nothing, to never be seen and to wake up in my bed and none of this has happened. You cannot be harmed here. I remember.

"In good time, you will be in bed again Ostara, in good time… maybe. If you make it out."

What? How? Did this voice just answer my thoughts? How is this even possible? I guess it is possible before I got into this cave. No, God no. I can't even hide my thoughts from this thing. It's all a dream. I am crazy. I am going crazy. Finally, the trauma has caught up with me and I am losing my mind. Maybe I am already dead. Maybe I have gone to hell. Is this hell? Maybe I am there.

The voice laughs a wicked laugh, the kind of laugh that sends shivers down your spine and curdles your stomach.

Arggghhh it is listening. I think to myself.

"Now, Ostara, I would really appreciate it if you didn't call me an 'it'. I have a name. My name is Helvac."

Helvac, right. Somehow the introduction of a name gives me a fraction of confidence to investigate further.

"Show yourself! If you want me to call you by your name then at least show me who and what you are!" I yell in the hope that I seem powerful through the fiery delivery of words.

A laugh ripples through the space again and I see a dark figure drop from somewhere above. I can't tell where from because this dark cave doesn't seem to have a beginning or an end.

This time I can see more detail. This Helvac character has short fur all over his or her body. I say him or her as it is almost genderless, but I think it's a him. His eyes are a deep yellow, almost golden. The weird thing is that even with the insane amount of confusion and fear in my body I manage to see the beauty of the gold in his eyes. His gold eyes sparkle slightly. But the rest of him. Oh God! The rest of him is terrifying. Scars riddle his body like a maimed lion after a lifetime of battles. His hands are claws and his nose is like a dogs nose, dripping with mucus. His ears are like decapitated horns, lumps in the side of his head, yet there is enough of a horn there to know they are horns. His mouth is black, his lips are black, everything is black, I can't tell if he has teeth or not. He stares at me as though he is giving me time to take him in. Weird. I feel a sense of gratitude to have this time to just take everything in as I feel like my world is spinning so fast and the sense of being overwhelmed is really what's alive in my body.

"Well, here I am," he says, opening his arms wide. Or whatever type of limbs they might be.

"I have been awaiting your company for quite some time, Ostara. I have lived many years here, in this place of The Unconscious, awaiting you to visit me," he says.

"I don't understand. If I have never met you before, how can you be waiting for me? What is this place? What is The Unconscious? What does that even mean to me?" I ask in desperation to orient myself and get some understanding of what is happening. "And what are you doing with this poor little girl?" I nod in the direction of the defeated child.

"Well, you see, we were sent here the moment you decided that you were powerless, a victim to your life. I was born to remind you, when you decided to come and visit. I am you,

51

Otstara. And that is also you." He replies, pointing to the defeated child. She raises her terrified little head and he is right. It IS me. She looks like me as a six-year old.

I laugh. I don't know why I am laughing. I should stop laughing. Not a good time to laugh. I can't help it. I guess it is a nervous response. He snarls at me. Ok stop laughing. Stop.

I hold my breath in the hope that I will pass out and wake up somewhere else, preferably at home.

Ok Ostara, get to the bottom of what's going on here so we can go home. I say to myself.

"How can you be me? I can see that she is me. You are over there I am here and you don't look anything like me. I don't have claws as hands and I sure as hell don't smell like burnt rotting flesh" I remark with fire.

I smell under my arms as I say that just to make sure I don't. "Nope, just like patchouli. Listen here buddy, I have no idea what you are talking about, but I have had one hell of a day so far with all this weirdness, so the best thing you could do is give me that child, or I will…" I trail off, a little unsure of just what I would do.

"You will what?" he smirks with his black, empty abyss of a mouth.

"I will… Will my way out of here. I don't know how but I will use my will. If this shit is happening to me then there must be a way. Where there is a will there's a way," I snarl. I am over this. I am done. I don't care what happens now. I just know I want to live.

"Now we are getting somewhere," he says.

What the hell. I think to myself. A sense of gratitude runs through my body for a moment as I feel a sense of getting somewhere. I would like to get out of here. That would be bloody great.

"Explain yourself," I demand.

Laughter echoes through the dense and never-ending space.

"I like that the fight is coming out in you, this is what I am inviting in you. The fight. The fight for you, your will, your power. I am your darkness, your shadows that lurk in every moment. You can't get rid of me you can only accept me.

"If the shadows go left unseen and unfelt I, Helvac will come back to haunt you, like in this very moment. To you I am haunting you, to me I am doing you a favour because you have been weak all your life, like this girl, weak. She bores me. I am trying to get some fight in her, that's what I am doing to her. Look at her. Weak. No one survives in life with such weakness, I need to beat it out of her," he says.

I take a moment to let the words sink into my mind. Flashes of memories flood my mind. Memories of my birth and the anger I felt towards my mother for leaving the earth when I was just a babe. Memories of when I fell as a child and I was shamed for making a mistake. Memories of my father losing his sense of self because of me. The anger, the deep violent rage I felt towards him for never seeing me. Memories of shame I felt when I desired something more in life, more magic and the voice inside my head tells me I am crazy. The shame. Memories of feeling unsafe in my life as though someone would cause me pain in any given moment, the fear I felt. Memories fill my mind and flow like a movie screen activating thoughts and emotions that are overwhelming. I see memories of myself curled over with my head in my hands just like this little girl, in defeat towards my own life. I remember her and in the moment that I remember her, I become her. I am now shackled to the floor in defeat. I feel the emotions flood my body like poison pulsating under my skin like an ache behind a bruise.

My breathing is sharp and heavy at the weight of feeling, feeling it all, this defeat, this self-hatred, this loneliness. I resist with everything I have to not let myself respond to such pain in my heart. I must fight it with everything I have. I must fight… him.

Without a second thought, I quietly bring myself to my feet in a crouched position in an attempt to go unseen. With anger in my body and determination in my mind I aggressively launch myself towards Helvac like a lion, arms spread out wide as I try to spear tackle him to the ground. My body aggressively jerks backwards and hits the floor so hard to makes my whole entire consciousness ring. Fuck. I forgot I was chained to the floor in my fit of rage.

Out of the corner or my eye I see Helvac start to circle me.

"I want your power," he says. "I want you to be alone forever. Here with me and only me, it's better that was. You are mine. Show me that you are worthy. Show me that you are worthy of me. I won't let you go anywhere until you give me what I want." He crouches down, closer to me and starts to whisper.

"I am wild,
Like the wind of a hurricane,
I am free,
Like the birds in the sky,
And the whispers they speak,
I am dark,
Like the night sky,
And the leather of the whip against your thighs,

I am powerful,
Like the roars of the underground,
I am fierce,
Like the crunch of teeth on your bones,
I am death and life at the same time,
I am harsh and cold,
Yet sweet and soft,
Like the dance of Helvac in the heavens,
I am the crash of thunder,
In the stormy skies,
And the gates to the Garden of Eden,
I am savage,
Like the tearing of your flesh,
As I turn you to stone,
I am remorseless,
In the face of tearing the world to the ground,
I am fearless in any battle in which I take part,
I am ruthless,
In the pursuit of success,
I do not care,
For the adversity that arises,
I do not whimper,
For the blood that pours from my body,
I do not shed the skin of my darkness,
I birth new layers,
New strength that is impenetrable,
I laugh at the face of death,

I embrace the limitlessness of endarkenment,
I do not descend into the depths,
As I am the depths from which I was born,
I am the void,
From where life emerges,
Like the womb of a mother,
I am the nothingness that is the everything,
Come and join me in hell, right here
Where fear is both born and diminished,
If you forget me, I will come for you,
I will scratch at your heart until you,
bleed from the inside out,
I will crunch on your bones until you fall to your knees,
I will tear you down and leave you empty,
Until you drown in your pain,
I will drain your lungs until you are left gasping for life,
You cannot fight me,
You cannot conquer me,
You cannot ignore me,
Try as you might,
You cannot prevail,
The more you fight me,
The tighter my grip of your lifeless body,
You cannot overcome me,
Like a baby cannot survive alone in the wild,
You can only submit to me,
I am your only choice,

When you choose me, I will set you free,
Without me you choose to be caged,
I am your darkness,
A leather hand held on your heart,
I am your wildest dreams
And your deepest fears,
I am your purest gold,
And your heaviest weight,
Your only choice is to invite me,
Because without me you won't exist,
Without me, you aren't you."

With the last words of his spell my body crumbles under the overwhelming pressure of the emotions rising through my now tiny little body.

You cannot be harmed here, call upon Tandarous when you need to, rings through my mind again.

Tandarous, I need you. I need you now my ally.

"Indeed, my friend, I am here for you," says a soft, but fearless, voice. This voice has a flavour of magic in it. I feel movement deep within my pelvis, like there is a snake circling from the base of my spine up into my heart and as it does it stirs the murky waters of the pain I was trying to control.

Without any control of my body, I open my mouth and I scream. I scream with every memory that is passing through my mind, every image I see; I scream. I throw my hands up in the air like I am drawing a dagger and I hit the ground, soft yet cold underneath me.

It is like I have no control over my body, my body is just speaking and moving me as the emotions rip through my entire being. I hit the ground repeatedly while I scream, it feels like the most natural thing to do with the anger. Daggers that I felt in the base of my being, my womb space and my stomach start to feel less painful, yet I can't stop. I can't stop hitting the ground with my little fists. The pain is starting to shift into a more pleasurable feeling. Pleasure. I haven't felt much of this in my life. Real pleasure like the kind you see in movies where the two characters are melted into each other in a trance state, their bodies moving in sync, and animal sounds escape them. I never thought I would feel that kind of pleasure in my lifetime. I thought it was only for fantasy or for magic people.

With the sensation of the pleasure comes deep shame again, shame that I am feeling this, shame that I am expressing like this, and I rip into the ground again. This time deep rage pours through me but towards myself. How did I not know what pleasure felt like, how could I be feeling pleasure in such pain. I feel shame to be human. Shame to have a disconnected home life. Shame to explore my sensual nature. Shame. More anger rages through my body. I take one last pummel of the ground as my body quakes, my breathing deepens and my chest opens. Pleasure rips through my body again, but not the sexual kind, the humble kind. This time the pleasure moves through me with grace, it dances and twirls and hits my stomach, right below where the top of my ribs meet. I feel this pleasure hit my stomach and it instantly makes me want to vomit, a sick feeling of anxiety floods me and I feel totally powerless as memories flood my mind again. Every moment in my life when I was powerless. Countless memories. There is a combination of shock and familiarity as I remember the moments I chose to be powerless. Times when I could have chosen to make a change in my life, when I could have asked for what I needed, when I could have said no instead of yes to things I didn't want to do. Memories of my most doomed and victim thoughts, suicidal thoughts, thoughts of the fucked-up-ness of the world. It is all here and slamming me in the face. I chose it all but I also chose not to see it... until now.

I tremble at the intensity of the anxiety in my stomach. I tremble, and the more I tremble I start to weep. Sounds of defeat escape my throat as I cannot hold onto the anxiety anymore, the more sounds escape the louder they become. The weeps turn into sobs. Yet the louder they become the more the anxiousness starts to subside. The soft relief starts to ripple in through the anxiousness like rain over a raging fire. Gently, softly dampening the damage. What feels like cool water showers my insides and relief is brought to my inner fire. My breathing slows and I feel my sternum pop open as I raise my head from the ashes that I created around me. My little child heart doesn't feel so childlike anymore as calmness has crept into my being. The water of my emotions swirls out through my heart. Blue magical mist pours out of my heart and the particles start to gather into an art form. A water dragon.

"Tandarous," I think to myself. I can feel her, she is my ally who initiated the ocean of feeling.

She bows her head to me in a combination of honouring and an agreement of what I said. This time I KNOW she can hear my thoughts. Like there is an obviousness that she can. No words needed. A simple acknowledgement as I bow to her. She has done this before. WE have done this before. I know it. It's a knowing that we are long lost friends.

Tandarous whips her tail and swiftly moves like a serpent around me and my ethereal body and the child version of me

59

melts together, we become one and I feel a deep sense of wholeness with her. This child is not alone anymore. I am here with her and she is here with me. As me. As one. No longer trapped in the past. She is free and I am free.

Within a moment of feeling an integration, a vision of Helvac flashes in my mind and I jump to my feet as I remember him. And then I see...

Helvac no longer looks like Helvac.

I curl back, stumble on my feet and drop to the ground.

Well, that's not what I was expecting.

Chapter Nine

The rebirth

Eyes like gold coins and with such depth, a level of magic that I have never seen before. Let's be real, this whole experience is nothing like I have experienced before, but these eyes… These eyes have a new layer of depth that is magnetic, almost hypnotizing. What once were claws are now nails but with a golden colour woven through, like the physical skin does not exist and his veins are made from gold. Fur that is a coat but a coat woven through his skin and the scars that were once like a maimed wild animal now look as though they are cracks in his skin, revealing a pulsating heart that is his etheric body. It is like cracks in a volcano, with golden lava breathing through to the rhythm of magic.

A mouth that looks as though it could be a portal into another world, into another dimension and it is something of magnificence. I have fallen to the ground in wonder, shock and mesmerisation I can't help but stare, just stare at what I had, only a few minutes ago, feared so deeply was going to kill me and eat me alive to never return home to Billie or my father again.

"Who are you now?" I ask in the search for a grasp on reality.

I get a cheeky smile in reply.

"I am still the same being, just not a creature anymore. I am still Helvac, I have transformed because you allowed me to, you allowed me to move through you and therefore I have transformed into something a little less… intimidating. You set me free. And just so you know… Helvac, my name means creativity, compassion, loyalty and generosity even though it may sound a little… well… hellish. You were simply experiencing the shadow side of that earlier," he says with another grin.

I take a deep breath and a hot minute to process everything he has just said. It feels weird calling him a him now because he looks so magnificent. An ethereal being from the heavens that only my mother would tell me about if she was here.

He laughs a loud laugh again. Damn it, I forgot he can hear my thoughts. Why can he do that?

"I can hear your thoughts because I am a version of you, Ostara. You are here in The Unconscious, because that is where you have been playing. For the last eight years of your life you have forgotten parts of yourself and buried them deep in the unconscious in order to navigate the world of the third dimension. You have forgotten your power, your anger, your rage, your sense of safety and your connection to everything.

"You have denied the humanness, the creature in you for far too long and with the denial, you have been choosing to live outside of your truth, your magic and your heart. Yes, the most savage parts of you are what you may deem to be scary or intimidating and something from a horror movie but all humans on this earth have these parts of them. You see, we are not separate, we are never separate, we are all reflections of each other. We are just a reflection of the greater consciousness that some people may call God and this greater consciousness has many layers, depths and heights including the darkness which is where we are now.

"The darkness is nothing to be feared, just something to be remembered and allowed to be, as for the many other layers. Your invocation here in The Unconscious is somewhat complete, you have allowed yourself to feel, to delve into the unknown of the rage, anger, fear, anxiousness and risen into the remembrance that when these emotions are felt, underneath it all is immense power that is a joy far greater than any avoidance that coaxes us away from our path.

"The whole point of being human is to feel, to experience, the whole spectrum of emotions, to accept the polarity of life and remember that in doing so you will always return to love, to joy and wholeness. The humanness is a storm to be ridden like a funfair ride in the knowing that with every feeling is a deepening, a realisation. Every feeling is an adventure of wholeness and Ostara you are here to bring the joy back into your human existence and therefore, return to wholeness."

Overwhelmed yet surprisingly ok, the words ring true in my heart, like I have heard this before. It makes sense. I am starting to get it. I just see, feel and know it is true somehow.

"Can you feel the lightness in your lower three centres? Can you feel how open they are now?" Helvac asks.

"Yeah, I can, its pleasurable, like a desire for life I have never felt before, or don't remember feeling," I reply.

"Yes! The last time you felt this desire was with your mother, in the womb of your mother," he says.

His words activate something in me. A remembering of my mother's words as she would speak to me in her womb. Remember joy, Ostara, remember that you are here to ignite joy in the world, starting with yourself. Ignite joy in every moment, even in the darkest of times. You are a warrior of light, especially when you forget, you will always find your way to remember.

There is a sense of lightness in my lower centres. A buzzing, but then it shifts and feels far away, yet so close and I remember my mother's ring that I found in her 'to be thrown out pile'. As I remember the ring I see a vision, clear as day, and I notice that the red, orange and yellow part of the ring is lit up, the colours have all become vibrant and fluorescent. The ring buzzes with energy and the more it buzzes the more I feel my mother's energy coming from each stone, an energy of confirmation that the words that are being spoken are truth, the words that my brain has so wanted to dismiss, actually this whole experience is something my logical brain wants to dismiss, but deep within my loins I can feel the truth within this wild journey that has felt like a lifetime.

"This ring was your mother's and she would use to journey into other realms to gather pieces of herself that she had forgotten. She was a warrior woman, yet she was so soft and gentle, she was a dream dancer, a walker in between worlds with a purpose to bring back truth into the world. This ring was her anchor into ascending through layers of herself back home to her true realm. Her purpose came to an end when you arrived into the world. Her duty was to deliver you here to experience your life as the great challenge it is and come home to yourself when the time aligned. She knew it was her time to return home, her mission was complete. It's now your turn Ostara, the time is now," Helvac explains.

I can't help but feel an excitement pulsate through my body as these words enter my brain, excitement melded with a small fear of failure. My brain runs. What if I can't do it? What if I am not strong enough to move through what I need to? What if I fail and let my mother and father down? I'll die if I fail.

"Are you listening to these voices in your head Ostara? The voices that are coaxing you away from this inner journey. This is the voice of your fear. Fear is to be felt but not to be acted on which only feds the beast. Remember what you just learned. If we act upon our fears, we make them reality. We ground the energy of fear into the world and that is not a world we are destined to create," Helvac explains.

I sigh. Having him listening to my thoughts isn't such a bad thing anymore. At first it was so intrusive but now it is helpful. Uncomfortable, but helpful. I guess I don't feel the need to hide anymore.

"That makes sense," I reply. "It all makes sense. Even in something that in my normal everyday life would seem so out of this world. If I ever told anyone of this experience, I would be dubbed crazy, even more weird than I normally am. Maybe they would even lock me up," I continue.

"Yes, perhaps," replies Helvac, with a chuckle in his voice. "But it is not up to you to care what others think, nor is it your job to focus upon how others perceive the world, your only duty is to focus on your true path… your heart. The rest will dissipate. Your true path is not the normal earth path, Ostara and it is not meant to be, you too are a dreamer," he continues.

I take a moment to allow this new information to land in my heart. Yes, I think to myself. Yes, this is the 'something more' that I was always thinking there was. I had always imagined that there had to be more to life than just following what had come before us, or what we were told we 'should' do in life. This is my path! The remembering of who I was before I came here to earth, remembering my soul purpose, remembering the essence of me so others can too. I feel my womb starting to pump full of blood, pleasure and excitement for the unknown that's coming. If I can feel to the depth of what I felt just minutes ago then I can tackle any task in front of me and I'll be damned if I would let the fear get the better of my journey back to… back to me and to each other.

"Annnnndddd there she is!" squeals Helvac as he claps his golden dust filled hands.

This is a side of him/me I haven't seen yet. He is sort of funny. Again, not what I expected but I guess that's where the magic is, in the unexpected.

"Are you ready to complete another step of your heart's journey?" he asks.

Without any hesitation I reply, "Yes. I am. Nervous, scared but ready. Ready as I'll ever be."

"To complete this part of your journey you need to merge with me and when we merge you will integrate all aspects of me. You will become one with me again and I will no longer be living in The Unconscious and forgotten world, we will be allies. You have a choice of how you would like to merge with me, this is a world of infinite possibilities so you can choose how you would love for it to unfold and once you merge with me you will enter into your next chapter. I cannot tell you what the next chapter will entail, nor when it will begin. That is for you to discover and to trust in yourself that, whatever arises and whenever the time is, you can manage it. If you ever feel as though you have forgotten, tap your chest and take a breath and remember to simply take the next step from your heart."

Helvac pauses to wait for my reply. I nod in agreement. Fear of the unknown fills my body, yet there is a pulsing in my womb that grounds me into my remembering, it's just a thread but it is powerful enough to keep me moving in choosing the next stage.

"I would like to hug you and merge with you. That's how I would love to enter my next phase. Hugs have always felt like home to me so that's what I am going to choose," I say.

Helvac nods in acknowledgment of my wishes.

"One last thing… Tandarous?" He calls her into my view. "You have made it through your first dominion, your first test, which means you now have your connection with your great protector, your dark weapon. This is your water Dragon, Tandarous." He says and he gestures towards her.

"I am your ally of the darkness, Ostara. No harm can come to you as long as you remember me. You will always be safe with me as I am a dragon and our gift is to protect the precious. I will always guide you to find the gold in any cave. You will need me in the future, not soon but in the future and no darkness may be placed upon you when I am with you," she says.

My mind wants to start predicting what I will need her for in the future but I set it aside in trust. "Thank you! I have always thought dragons are so badass. Thank you for being my ally. You have granted me one of my lifelong wishes of having a sister!" I glee.

"Great, now, whenever you are ready take a few deep breaths and walk into my arms. Always remember that you can do this. Just believe you can and you will. Thank you for seeing me and setting me free," Helvac says as he opens his arms in an invitation to merge with him.

"You are welcome," I smile in appreciation and gratitude that I could set some part of me free. I nod in honour to Tandarous and I take steps towards Helvac. I wrap my arms around him and he feels warm and electric. It is the most intense sensation of love I think I have ever experienced.

I gasp in response to the electric sensations that fire in my body, my body melts and Tandarous tornadoes herself around us and washes us with her watery body then I feel a pop around me and everything turns white.

Chapter Ten

The Heart

It's warm here, an eery stillness, yet warm and inviting. All I can see is white, white that goes for miles and miles with no end. No start, no finish, no bottom, no top, a huge light feeling of nothingness that feels like everything as well. Strange. It's a day for it.

If this was some kind of heaven then it would most definitely be what I had pictured… There are no smells here, no wind, it's so still, yet I don't feel fear like I felt in the last place, or should I say, The Unconscious. I wonder what this place is called? And how weird that this place doesn't have a voice that speaks over a big announcement speaker like The Unconscious. What am I meant to do here? This seems weird. I have a task to do, to complete and I can feel it in my nuggets that it is somewhat important here so I would like to start getting on with it.

Another part of me just wants to take it all in and relish in the calmness of it all, yet this new activation that I feel from the last place is firing up like a furnace waiting to go on an adventure to find whatever I need to find here. Hell, I had no idea I would get injected with a passion fire from the last place so who knows what will go on here.

I feel my finger buzz, somehow I am wearing my mother's ring. I can't remember putting it on. I mean, I didn't. I must have somewhere in between these worlds. Or Helvac did. He must have and I am ok with that. It looks good on me. As I am looking down at my mother's ring I can see that the pink and blue crystals are flickering.

Something is coming. Something is going to happen. I feel like I am in a video game, like I am the character feeling everything but also being the player of the game. In the game but not of it.

My heart starts to race a little as I feel nervous of the unknown and I am still so damn unsure of this stillness. Why is it so still?

My ears prick up as I hear a tiny sound of something coming from somewhere. I focus. It sounds like a child is crying. I close my eyes and I squeeze them shut, then I squint in the hopes it will give my hearing superpowers. Yeah, good one, Ostara, like that's going to work.

I hear it again, yet this time it is a little louder. Great! Squinting works! Focus = superpowers, great, noted.

I hear the sob of a child and this time the sound is much closer. I open my eyes to search the space. I spin around from right to left quicker than I have ever spun before, I almost make myself dizzy. Alright Ostara, you are no use to any child here if you aren't focused. Take a deep breath and relax a little.

I slowly turn around, searching the entire space thoroughly and there it is. In the far distance, a tiny little figure is floating. It looks as though it is floating as everything is white so there is nothing that seems tangibly up or down. It is trippy that's for sure. If I ever do drugs I am sure that this is what it would be like. I feel my heart start to beat a little faster. Phoar, this is gonna be something, better start thinking of the exit plan. I hear my brain pipe up. Well brain hasn't this whole thing been a 'something'? Pipe down please and let me focus.

No exit plan, Ostara, the only exit plan is forward, just keep moving forward, move through it like I moved through the last. One foot in front of the other. Let's go.

One foot starts moving, my breathing is slowing and deepening. All we've gotta do is breathe in deep and slowly exhale. Oh boy that feels good. Why don't I do that more often, breathing seems like the easiest thing we do as humans yet the thing we have forgotten, well at least now I have realised I have. I wonder if all humans have forgotten to breathe? I must not be the only one. I realise that the world we live in is really a place of disconnect, a place where we have forgotten the simplest, most fundamental of things.

One foot in front of the other, that's what I am telling myself yet I feel like I am floating on a cloud. If we could walk on clouds I am sure that this is what it would feel like, I am certain of it. As I move closer to the tiny little figure I start to see that it is a small child, yet this small child looks as though she is hidden behind a dark curtain. Her clothes are torn, her skin is dirty, her hair is dark and she is rocking back and forth as though she is in the midst of a psychotic break. As I move closer I start to pick up her smell; she is musky, like she has been sitting in a dark room for ten years and her clothes have become mouldy. She looks terrified, traumatised and I feel this overwhelming maternal need to protect her.

"Hey there," I say in a soft and gentle voice as I try not to frighten her more than she already is.

She gasps and while turning to face me she also starts trying to move away from me, slowly. It's as if she thinks I am here to hurt her. I stop in my tracks as I don't want to scare her even more.

"It's ok, I'm not here to hurt you. I am here to…" I pause, not quite sure what to say. "I am here to listen," I continue.

71

Her head tilts slightly as she takes in the information. Her eyes open and she looks me in the eye with curiosity, like an abandoned puppy being given loving attention for the first time.

"Listen?" she asks.

"Yes, I am here to listen to you. I would love to know how you are feeling and what is going on for you?" I say. The words escape my mouth without even knowing why I said them. I guess it just feels right.

She wriggles in her seat a little as she has her arms wrapped around her legs, like an upright foetal position.

"What is your name?" I ask.

She looks at me as if she is trying to work out if she should be telling me her name. I think she is weighing up if I am a threat or not. She is so scared and unsure of me. Am I really that scary? Boy, I wonder what happened to this poor girl.

"My name is Ostara," she says.

What the fuck. I think to myself. This is not a coincidence. And then I remember what Helvac had said to me about reflections. I mean if I could take anything from this whole experience I may as well learn from the last world I was dragged into. Ok, so if Helvac was a version of me then it makes sense that this little girl is a version of me too.

I don't remember ever wearing a nightgown like that though, and I never remember being that dirty, but I guess I will have to go with it. Ostara is not a common name, I have never met anyone else with the same name so I know that this is another lesson right here for me.

Ok Ostara, be of service to this version of you. Ok, I choose to be of service to the highest good of Ostara, I choose the end result of guiding her back to love and I choose to come from my heart. I take a few deep breaths after learning how great that makes me feel.

"That's a really beautiful name. My name is Ostara too. It is nice to meet you."

She looks at me with a very puzzled look on her face, just as I had felt when she told me her name.

"Is it ok if I sit down with you, Ostara?" I ask.

She nervously nods her head. She wants my company but is also terrified of it.

"I would love to know how you are feeling. I can go first in sharing if you like, just so you can also feel me too?" I say.

"Yes, I would like that," she replies.

"I am feeling a little overwhelmed by the last few experiences I have had today, it has been quite a big day full of lots of learnings and new experiences that I could have never made up in my mind. I have been going through quite a few different emotions that I hadn't felt so intensely for a long time. It has been an overwhelming day, yet I feel a sense of accomplishment in my heart, like I am connected to love no matter what, even through the pain, love still lingers. So, to cut a long story short; I am feeling a lot. How are you feeling?" I ask.

"I feel scared. Frozen," she replies.

Ok, what would a mother say right now, Ostara? Heart. Speak from your heart.

"Thank you for sharing that with me. It is fair enough you are feeling so scared, it is valid. What is it that is scaring you?" I ask as softly as I can.

"I am scared of…" she pauses. "Out there," she says gesturing her hands in a wide arc.

"Out there? Do you mean out there, the world?" I ask.

She nods slowly, but manically. Her eyes glaze over as if her soul has left her body and she can't deal with the thought of the outside world. *Wow ok, this might take a little longer than I thought.* I think to myself.

Bow down to her greatness. I hear a voice say. Oh, there we go, there *is* a voice here, it just hasn't spoken yet. The voice reminds me of my mother's. Soft and warm like butter.

Take a moment to acknowledge her greatness, she is a scared child who only knows the fear she is in right now. The fear is her whole world. Can you take a moment to acknowledge that she is more than her fear so she can see it too?

Pain hits my heart like someone has just shot an arrow into my chest. I remember. I can feel the voice. The voice of my mother. A remembrance enters my being and with the remembrance comes deep pain and anguish. The arrow in my chest gets heavier as I try to ignore it. I try to ignore it for the betterment of this child who is a version of me. She is already so traumatised so I can't let her see me in pain, she will be so frightened. Put on a brave face, I tell myself.

The voice echoes through my being again.

Don't you think that this little girl needs permission to feel her own pain? Don't you think it would be powerful for her to see you feeling your own pain so she can remember to feel hers?

Pain. Deep pain. Memories flood my mind again without my control. Memories, like a video on fast forward, cascade into my consciousness. My chest. All of the thoughts I have ever had about myself come to the surface. You will never be good enough. You are unworthy of love. You will never be perfect. You were never good enough for your dad. You were never capable enough to change the world and you never will be. You aren't allowed to have everything you desire. You are not powerful enough. Who do you think you are? Your mother left you because there is something wrong with you. You are a disgrace to this world. YOU KILLED YOUR MOTHER!

I try to overcome the intensity of these thoughts with breathing. Breathe, breathe, breathe.

This time I hear the voice whisper; 'Breathe and listen, listen to your heart. She wants to cry. Listen to your soul when she wants to heal. Listen to your power when she wants to reclaim her authority in living her life. Listen'

A single tear escapes my eye as I start to let go. I let go of the need to control myself. I let go of a forced sense of having it all together at sixteen. I let go of parenting my own parent and letting myself crumble in the madness of my mind. My arms automatically come into my chest as if to hold my heart and I let out a whimper. The feeling of holding myself activates a desire to let go and be wild and free in this animalistic pain. This time it feels different. This time I just want to let myself feel defeated in life. I feel my body crumble into a similar position as little Ostara on the floor.

I wrap my arms around my legs and rock backwards and forwards. A second tear drops and my whimper gets louder. The whimper becomes a sob. The sob becomes a wail.

As I deepen into the pain in my heart, memories arise, memories from my childhood of the times when I had to hold myself, do my crying to myself, when Dad wasn't there for me. When he was too far into his own disillusion that he would forget to care for my needs. Memories of the judgement I received from his eyes without him intending it but I could feel it. I could feel that he would have rather had my mother than to have me and a big part of him blamed me for her death. I sob. A wave of heat fires through my body and carries through my heart. With every sob and every sound the pain starts to fizzle like bacon on a hot plate. It starts to melt. Deeper. She says. Deeper. What's underneath it all?

A vision slaps me in the face harder than Muhammad Ali punched his opponents. I think I would prefer to have been punched in the face because the memory hurts more.

The vision floods my eyes, I want to unsee it, I want to get away from it. I don't want to experience this. So painful. I see my mother and her big round belly with me inside it, like X-ray vision I can see it all. I see me rolling around and moving as my mother speaks as she realises all of what is going on. My mother was a clear channel for something greater than what humans would comprehend as normal. My mother in this vision is speaking with her eyes closed and she paints a picture of such beauty and grace, the energy she holds is something truly magical. She stands in the paddock in which I was born, barefoot and connected with the earth, her heart is open and she has light pouring from the top of her head. Her hands are open towards the space in front of her, as if inviting something in, inviting someone to come and give her a hug. I listen and I watch as I want to know what happens next, I want to know why I am being shown this image. It's an image, yet it feels like a memory. I see my mother's mouth moving as if she is speaking to someone. I know she is speaking to something out of this world. My father always said she was woo woo like that. She is and was the greatest channel of all time. She nods as if coming to an agreement on something. Zoom in, I hear her say. I zoom in on the memory and I see tears streaming down her face, I feel a heartbreak in her that sends shivers down my spine. She aches, yet there is a fierceness to her acceptance. I see a golden thread that streams from her heart, through the top of her head and into the clouds. She brings her hands down to her heart and lets out a sob of grief. I can see baby me inside her belly respond to the grief that washes over her body, I roll and I kick in an attempt to let her know I am there. She brings her hands down to her belly and weeps.

What is going on? I want to understand!

Zoom in, I hear her say again. Listen to my thoughts, in this space you can, you can access all information through all time and space. Imagine that you already know.

I zoom in on the vision, onto the baby version of me who is swirling around in my mother's belly. I shift into the perspective of me as a baby and I remember, I see and I feel it all.

Even as a baby I too heard the words that my mother was receiving from the higher worlds. I too experienced her pain and grief as the knowledge of her death to come was passed down. My mother held a deep acceptance for this truth, almost as though there was some excitement that her duty is being served but deep grief for the knowing that she would not get to see her daughter grow up, take her first steps, say her first word, or experience the bond of a mother and daughter over the years.

I too feel this as I am living the perspective of baby me in a womb. I grieve knowing that I will not have a mother. I hear the knowledge that my mother will pass over into the light after she passes me over to the earth side. As a baby I notice that I hear this information and know it means that her death will be my fault. Her death will be on me even as a baby in the womb. And because of that, I decided as a baby that I cannot exist in the world because if I exist in the world I will create pain everywhere I go, no matter what. What a sad choice to make.

As the realisation ripples through my mind and clarity drops; the vision of my mother and baby me fades and I come back to my body still on the floor yet now I am lying flat with my arms spread out, heart open, surrendered and simply weeping. Giving myself full permission to acknowledge the humanness in me, the baby in the womb who told herself she can't exist in the world because she will create pain. I weep for the baby in me. I weep for her humanness and all the times she has not gone for what she loves because she tells herself she will create pain in doing so. I weep at the pain of all the times I remember rejecting love, rejecting friends, rejecting my father because I can't receive love because I believed I was creating pain. I have created it with the choice I made.

I allow myself to feel it all and for some reason I know I need to keep my arms open, it feels good to do so like I am letting go of it all.

I cry, sob, remember the memory and cry again. Until. I slowly stop and relief fills my body.

Chapter Eleven

The Remembering

I remember the other little Ostara that is still in this space and my eyes fly open faster than the thought can process. I am feeling lighter, much lighter and I feel a sense of joy for remembering the depth from where I came, the story of me. The depth of my pain. I can feel this sense of knowing that in this feeling I can access a deeper level of love and understanding for myself, others and the world.

I sit up like a shot as I feel this sense of responsibility for Ostara who I abandoned for who knows how long while I was in yet another vision. A vision within a vision, an inception. It is the strangest of thoughts to have but I feel more at home than I ever have. At home in this remembering of the stories I made up as a baby simply from the pain I had experienced. I feel a tender understanding and with that, peace.

I turn to see Ostara in the same place I left her but she is sitting in a different position. She looks more comfortable, like she is no longer frightened of me.

"Hey," I say in a gentle voice. Hey is all that I can get out right now.

She smiles at me. Only a slight smile but I will take it.

"I am sorry for going somewhere else just then. I just needed a moment to just be with me to better understand myself so I can better understand you," I say.

"I know, I could hear your thoughts," she replies.

Damn another one who can hear my thoughts, I think to myself and she giggles.

"Well, it is nice to see you smiling, Ostara. How are you feeling now?" I ask.

"I am feeling hopeful," she replies.

"Hopeful? Hopeful for what?"

"Hopeful that you will listen now," she says.

I look at her with puzzlement.

"I am willing to listen, I promise. I am ready to listen right now," I say.

She smiles. She is still dirty but she is more relaxed. She looks so cute in her ragged clothes. She ushers herself a little closer to me as if she is going to whisper and tell me a secret. "I was sad because you never listened, I would cry out to you in times when I wanted love, when I wanted to speak my mind and ask for what I needed. I would cry out to you, send you messages and whisper in your ear when I was terrified of existing in the world. All I wanted was a moment of your attention. All I wanted was some time from you. It feels nice when you let me express, when you let me exist in the world through feeling. All I want is for you to listen, to feel and to express me. I am hopeful you will. Hopeful," she says.

I sigh. So wise. I get it. I get it now. She is my heart, my heart's expression and I have locked her away all this time. I sigh again. "I am sorry I ignored you and locked you away. I promise that I will listen from here on in. I promise," I say.

She nods in acceptance of my declaration to her.

"Is there anything I can do for you to prove my willingness to choose you?" I ask.

"Do you remember when we would be playing on the floor with blocks and building something so great like a house that was almost a castle and Daddy would never notice? We would repeat Dad over and over but he was in his own world?" she asks.

"Yes, I do remember that, I remember that happening often. Why do you speak of this?" I ask.

"Well, these are the times that I needed your attention, these are the times when I needed you to stop and remind me of what I am worth and that my worth is not dependent on someone outside of myself. That's when I needed you to parent me. Dad was never the parent, he doesn't need to be. I am the one who is in need of parenting by you. You, the older version of me," she responds.

What wisdom I think to myself. Damn I am mesmerised by a child who is spitting out all kinds of wisdom. How come I don't think of that kind of shit. It makes sense. She is the child version of me, the part of my heart that is in pain so of course the child version of me needs a parent, a friend, an ally. Of course, the child version of me is needing some love and presence from me. Just like Helvac. I get it now!

She smiles at me in response to my thoughts.

"You get it now. This is nice. Does this mean that you will honour my request of being listened to?" she asks in such an eloquent way.

"Yes, Ostara. I promise to listen. I promise that whenever I feel you cry out for attention, when my emotions arise and I need a moment to speak with you, I will. I will come here into this space of heart and speak with you. I will spend some time with you to hear the wisdom of what you need to say and the visions that you need to offer me in order for me to rise to the occasion. I promise," I say.

Although she is still dirty and in her ragged clothes her energy is shifted tenfold. She is no longer in fear of the world coming to get her because she is not allowed to exist there, she is no longer afraid of me, she is a somewhat normal child. What a shift. All because I gave myself a moment to feel. Magic really is real.

"Can I give you a hug Ostara?" I ask.

She beams with a big cheesy grin. Her eyes are dark and her hair is a little messy but she has the most beautiful grin. She is sunshine personified. If she had cleaner clothes then she would look like a princess of the sun.

Remember this place is magic Ostara, anything is possible here. If you want to give her princess clothes, you can do that if you want. I hear my mother's voice echo through my mind.

Oh of course. If I can have experiences of being a child and witness beings miraculously transform in front of me then of course I can choose clothes for my little me.

"Ostara, would you be open to the idea of me giving you some princess clothes? I feel as though you are a sunshine princess and I would love to honour you as that by giving you some beautiful clothes," I say.

Before I even finish my sentence she is already beaming and nodding ferociously in excitement. I giggle in response to her joy. It's hard not to.

I close my eyes and take a deep breath. Mum, can you guide me? I haven't done this before. I ask inside my mind.

"Take a moment to connect to your heart, place a hand on your heart, take a few deep breaths and set the intention to be of service to the highest good. Take another deep breath. Then choose the end result of gifting Ostara with clothes of a princess and imagine her in front of you with princess clothes. Imagine it and choose it. Choose this for her and see her in her greatness. Take a few deep breaths and sink a little deeper into your heart." She pauses. "Now open your eyes".

Low and behold. There she is, looking like a princess. A sun princess with a golden tutu like a sunflower and a little golden crown. Not too over the top. Just how we like it, well just how I imagined it. Her hair is clean and the greyness to her skin has popped and her beautiful, vibrant, pale skin has come through. She is so pale she almost reflects light, it's intense for my eyes.

She is so excited by her new clothes.

"You know exactly what I wanted to wear! Yellow is my favourite colour and I LOVE sunflowers," she beams.

"I know, because they are my favourite too," I reply with a smile.

"Give me a twirl," I say while gesturing with my finger.

She twirls around and begins to dance. Of course, I have to join in. Dancing is my jam! Without any thought I jump up to dance with her. She is so beautiful when she dances. So free. So wild and so innocent. She is beautiful. A reflection of how the entire world could be in every moment with a conscious choice. How I could be in every moment if I simply choose. Right now, I am choosing it. Choosing to feel the joy that weaves through every moment in life, even if sometimes I forget. I am human, I forget and I can equally as easily, remember.

Giggles echo through the vastness of this space. My heart feels open, full and surrendered. I twirl and move my feet in all directions as I mirror little Ostara's funky moves. She laughs at my attempt to be as funky as she is. I laugh at the thought of me trying to be funky in the first place but not in a self-downgrading way, in an accepting way; that maybe funky isn't the best descriptive word for me. Abstract. That's the best word for me. I smile at the thought of that word. Abstract, I am.

I take a moment to let this moment sink in. I close my eyes and take a deep breath right into my belly. My chest and heart expand as I allow as much air in as I can so I can let more of this moment land in my being. I open my eyes and I see my mother standing in the near distance with a beautiful smile on her face. I can smell her. I always remember her smell. Lavender and honey, such a peaceful smell. She is wearing what I always imagined her to be wearing, a floral skirt and white button up top that is loosely fitted. She likes to be free in her movement like me, loosely fitted was always her thing. I don't know how I remember that but for some reason here in this space I remember. Her golden wavy hair falls down the sides of her face and her soulful brown eyes penetrate mine. She penetrates me with love and presence. I notice that I don't feel the pain in my heart as I see her this time, this time I feel gratitude for this moment of connection, this time I feel joy in seeing her. The pain, the anger, the resentment has subsided and morphed into appreciation. I smile softly as realisation of what is possible when I let the magic of my truth flow, when I let myself meet all versions of me. For the first time in my sixteen years of being on the earth, I feel at ease. I feel more home than I have been in a long time. I bask in this moment and hold my mother's gaze powerfully, never wanting to let go of this moment.

"Thank you," I whisper.

She bows her head to me in response and whispers, "No, thank you."

She brings her hand to her mouth to blow me a kiss and when she does she blows a golden mist into my face and I feel my world change again.

Chapter Twelve

The Becoming

My eyes are closed and my senses are heightened. My body feels as though it almost doesn't exist, as if I am floating in a sea of nothingness. So calm. It is as if when I move my ethereal body I can feel ripples of frequency waves coming off it in a sea of consciousness. Where am I? I think to myself. I want to know, but I also don't feel the need to know. It's a neutral feeling and I like it. Complete peace. There are no heightened emotions in any direction, good or bad. There is a calm here like the waters of a pond on a breeze-free day.

I open my eyes and what is in front of me is nothing I have ever seen in reality before, only in my imagination, only in my dreams, only in the things that most humans deem to be 'not real'. Right here, right now, this is so real. The most real feeling of being home, home in a place I have never seen or been before. There are stars above me and around me. I see a many different expressions of stars, all different colours, shapes, sizes. I see galaxies that are like a vortex of energy, planets in the distance all around me, some so big that they take up almost the whole sky. Some purple, some blue, some gray, it is like I have entered a comic book, it is all just so... so much. So extra. I see the moon as it floats in the darkness yet it shines so bright in the reflection from the multiple suns that are what seems to be light years away. I had never thought we had more than one sun but here I am wrong.

Have I really just entered heaven? Below my feet I feel the softest grass and the most moist moss I have ever felt. It feels like I am standing on a velvet rug of joy, I cannot help but dance my feet from left to right to feel the soft sensation of cold moist most brush over my feet in pleasure. I breathe into the deepest parts of me right down into my feet to take in a moment that feels like everything.

Who knows, anything is possible here in the imagination. I guess that's where I am, it's the only suggestion I have that makes sense. There is a shallow pond of water just below the mossy rock on which I stand, that stretches far into the most glorious green garden. It could be the Garden of Eden. Fresh and flourishing roses, flowers and nature are teeming with life. There are moths and butterflies that look electric, like something out of Avatar, flying around suckling on the most beautiful and wholesome flowers. Most are strange and unique creatures that do not live on earth as we know it today. Some bugs with wings of birds and butterfly-like creatures with wings that look like they belong to stingrays. It is warm here, like the sweetest and warmest hug I have ever had and I am filled with hope and wonder. Could this world be possible for humans? There are small creatures that dance around each other as they journey on to what they are seeking. It is a picture of pure magic. I am in a world of Avatar without it being a movie. It a world I would love to live in.

I wiggle my feet to test the waters and sure enough a water like energy ripples off my feet and it keeps going for as far as I can see. *That's cool.* I have been to places like this but only in my imagination. I always had this thing about going on imaginative journeys to explore and see if I could connect with non-terrestrials or aliens as most call them. All of the aliens I have met always told me they are not alien, they are not extra, they are just non-terrestrials and that's what they prefer being called, but I always thought that I was making this up, ya'know how your parents always tell you that whatever you are imagining is what you are just making up and isn't real. I wonder how I am going to tell my dad about this one. I am sure he would say something like, "You are just like your mother aren't you," and pat me on the head like a well-behaved puppy. Perhaps I won't share this one with him, or anyone for that matter. This whole journey has been crazy but if I tell anyone about floating in a watery bubble of heaven on earth, I will be totally ostracized and kicked out of the world, never allowed to exist. Maybe even Dad will kick me out, regardless, this seems out of this world. Literally… and I like it. It abstract, like me.

This place is beautiful. All kinds of purples and blues are painted through the skies and stars full of rainbow colours are etched everywhere in what looks like a ceiling of cosmic magic. If only I could take a picture and bring it back home to show people what it really looks like here. It is strange that when I move my feet it feels like I am wading through water and the entire multi-verse responds, the creatures, the forest, the skies, it is all effected by my movement. It's like I am sending out wave signals with every step, it is like it is all completely connected, nothing separate, nothing asleep, it's all listening all the time. The inner child in me wants to take over and see how I can play with this cool wave signal thing. I remember what little Ostara from the last world had told me. "Remember to listen to me". So that's what I am going to do.

I imagine a funky beat in my head and I start clicking my fingers, then sounds start coming from my mouth to make a tune. Babadadadum baba, babadadadum babaaa. My head starts bobbing. My hips start swaying and my feet start tapping. Here we go I think to myself, this is fun. The music in my mind becomes tangible and I start feeling it pulse through my body, waves of joy, waves of delight and ease penetrate through me. I feel it like you feel it when you stand right next to a speaker at a concert and it vibrates your whole body. The sensory experience is flooding through me. I close my eyes and let it move me, I let go, I surrender and let little Ostara play. I peak one eye open to see what waves of frequency are coming off my body and this time instead of just seeing waves I see different coloured waves, a whole rainbow of colours and each colour has a different pattern, a different shape like an imprint or a code. Now this is really fun and I want to play even more with this newfound game. I wonder if I change the movements of my body and dance with different emotions, will I see even cooler patterns. I take a deep breath, scrunch up my face to make an angry face and stomp my feet like a Viking going to battle, it takes me back to when I was hanging out with Helvac. Only this time I am really enjoying the expression of my inner Viking, my inner angry warrior. As I embody this energy I see red waves with spiky patterns fly off and out from my feet and pelvic region when I am stomping. Different emotions have a particular expression of themselves. That's a mind-boggling thought. Ok I will try something different. I will try something a bit more painful. I take a moment to think of my mother and the perspective I was in when I went back to the memory of being a baby and I feel the grief come in. Instantly I notice blue energy balls that start to come out of my heart, but these energy balls are a little static. I jump up and down and shake my body to shake off that energy, we have already gone through that one. Let me see what sensual energy looks like. I begin to touch all over my body, I let my hands slide across my body, my face, my womb, my chest and I let a surrendered feminine energy take over my body, breathing deeply into as many cells as I can and this time I see orange colours shaped as a flower vibrate out of my body and into the expansiveness but the flowers dance and swirl around. It is so beautiful to witness. What an art form these energies are. I never want to leave this place, there is so much to explore here. So much to see and to experience.

I feel joy take over my body and I let it, I dance, I jump around, I squeal with joy, I let myself play like a child in a magical place that I am somehow experiencing in such realness. I watch the colours and patterns fly from my body like a rainbow dance party and let it all spread out into the vastness of the cosmos. I dance to the beat in my mind and I move to the joy in my body.

Surrendered, playful and at home in my body. At peace even in the strangeness. None of that matters. None of it matters when the heart is present. If I am learning anything from this space in the cosmos it is that all energy comes and goes and underneath it all is peace, the joy of feeling the whole spectrum of emotions and that every single emotion has its own imprint of expansion. When we let the emotions be fully expressed then we have the choice to come home to joy, to this. *Woah.* I think I just blew my own mind with my own wisdom. I have no idea where that came from. I guess I am wise.

I close my eyes and let my own wisdom sink in as I spread my arms wide and spin around in circles. My body is moving in all kinds of directions and I love it, like one of those air men that are outside of car yards to get your attention. That's what I imagine myself to look like at this very moment. Totally lost in myself and in the magic of this moment. Totally lost in the joy of my own heart and my own expression.

Mmm home. I think to myself. Home is where the heart is.

And then I feel a presence enter the space that is not my own.

Chapter Thirteen

Sankai

She dances like the wind and moves like the swiftest of beauties I have ever seen. So wild and free yet so tender and soft. Her spirit is so strong and her heart's boundaries are softening like a marshmallow roasting on a fire. I see her walls around her soul dissipating the more she steps into her own sovereignty. Ahhhh this is what I love to see. I have watched her since the moment she was born. I watched her blossom and grow and fall and get back up again. I have witnessed her go through pain and tribulations and how her monkey mind built walls around herself to protect the softness of her emotion. The earthly world is a place that is slowly enlightening to the thought of sharing true emotion, slowing transitioning into a space of acceptance. Slowly, ever so slowly. My hope is that Ostara will be one who brings home the magic of expression, the magic of what it is to live in their heart, regardless of all trials and tribulations. One can only hope that she will listen to her own heart and expression to guide others home to theirs. Her mother, such a soul who did much work with us in the cosmic realm, dedicated her life to the greater good of humanity and what it means to live from the heart. Her last sacrifice was herself. Knowing that she had to allow the hardest of tribulations to befall her, so her star seed daughter could transform through pain and find the path back home. And in that journey, she would teach others to do the same through the lessons she would learn along the way.

I am Sankai. My name means the guide of the light. I am here to be the guide to a light soul who will lead the way in the remembrance of joy, wonder and faith of what is truly possible when one is connected to the heart. Joy is the whole point of being human. Evil is upon us and will always have a way of making its presence known here on earth. Our only job is to remember the joy and stay connected to our souls. One thing that can never be taken away is our soul's essence, our hearts' truth. My faith is that Ostara will be one who will teach others the importance of expression, of letting go of the ties we have to our ego's agenda of fear and limitations. My hope is that she will forever remember her connection to source and show others theirs too.

My world here in the galactic portal is not of the earthly realm, as we see all, know all and feel all of what it is to be existing through all time and space. I have followed Ostara since birth and I was the one who sent her here to Earth to serve her duty. A spirit guide, or cosmic servant is what some may call beings like myself. I serve the one consciousness in the ascension of humanity into full ownership of all.

We in the galactic portal also have planets, star systems and galaxies that we call home. Where our species thrive and also have evil who wants to engulf our magic and take it away. We too, like humans, have a purpose to serve. Many of us have multiple different humans to attend to, to energetically push in the direction of what is true for them. Unlike humans we are not limited in time as time is only a construct of the human mind to understand their reality as the ego always seeks orientation in the earthly realm. Here in the cosmos we can jump through timelines, step through into different worlds as we choose. Intention is everything, our intention leads us to wherever we need to go, our intention is the tension that catapults us into the reality, time or space we choose to go to. Humans are much the same, yet they have not realised it yet as they are still learning to connect to their own true heart that weaves through everything they do. The joy is an extension of the actions they take from their heart. The cosmic joke is this; when you take actions from the truth of your heart you are not only serving yourself in the highest good but also serving the world as a living and breathing organism as well as the entire galactic force and source consciousness. Humans have been enslaved by their monkey mind as dark forces have manipulated and tortured their minds to believe they are unsafe and separate so they unconsciously put the trust and power outside of self. This brought great sadness to the cosmic realms. Humans fell asleep to their connection to themselves and to us here in the cosmos. All humans have great ability to communicate with us and allow us to guide them, yet their fingers are in their ears and their hands are over their eyes so they cannot hear or see. This can be reversed with the remembrance of connection to all time and space and in turn connection to peace. Even though I am not human, I can see, feel and understand what it means to be one.

My duty here with Ostara is to engrain my world back into her human experience. The secret that has never been revealed is that everything in the world is connected by a web, a web of light energy that binds everything into a tight knit web of creation. Even others on the opposite side of the world have a connection and can energetically tap into another. Even other beings from outer space like me are always connected and communicating with beings that are terrestrial. The lines of communication are always there to be tapped into. It's like a telephone that can always be picked up and spoken through to anyone in the world. This is a secret that is not a secret, it is a long known magical practice that dark forces have dampened in the fear of losing control of the masses. My job is to allow Ostara to remember her connection and share that with the world. My job is to bring humanity home. My first step is Ostara.

Chapter Fourteen

The Awakening

I feel a presence that seems familiar yet also strangely out of this world. I stop my dance movements like a game of musical chairs when the music stops and my eyes fly open. I sigh out in remembrance of an old friend. I recognise this soul. And that she is… a soul. Not quite of the human world, she is beautiful; like a graceful energy ball that has morphed into a being.

She sparkles with different colours, almost vibrating with excitement as she sees that I remember her. She is very celestial looking. No hair. Almost genderless, yet somehow I know she is a female. Her hands have slightly bulgy fingers at the end and her feet dissolve into the ether, they aren't quite there. She floats in front of me.

It's the most humbling experience to be a witness to such beauty and magic. Perhaps I am only in my imagination, perhaps I am only in the land of crazies and I should be sent away, but it sure as hell doesn't feel that way. This moment, this time, feels more like a remembering of my home than ever before. This being feels more like home to me than any other human I have interacted with, even Billie. She feels like a part of me that I never knew existed. She moves like me, she dances like me, wild and wonderful, different and sparkly, strange and outrageous, yet soft and present. Even though I have not experienced all these flavours of her I somehow know that I have, in past lifetimes, in past dreams.

This sight is something only the human superconscious could ever dream of. It is as though she is a blueprint of my spirit. That is certainly how it feels to meet her. This time, I have no doubt that she can hear my thoughts, it is as though she is an expression of my thoughts. So, I think to myself, but to her at the same time.

"Hello, it is so nice to meet you," I think.

"Hello, Ostara it is so nice to be communicating with you so clearly. I am glad you have chosen to come home," she replies.

"I am not completely sure what that means but I am sure I will find out. I would love to know what this is all about. I have been through two earlier worlds, but this feels like the end. Not the end as in I will never come back, but the end of the journey I have been on. This feels like the highest of experiences and perspectives that I could possibly reach. Am I right?" I ask.

She smiles. "You truly have returned. In the cosmic realm you are always connected to everything through all time and space and you have access to any information you need. Most humans call this the Akashic records. The Akashic records don't belong to one place in the cosmos, it is a part of everything in the universe. Right now, right here you are experiencing the cosmic realm in a very tangible way which most have denied within themselves to ever experience again. This is your last stop before you return to your human body, back to Billie and back to your father. But we have much to discuss before you return home," she says telepathically.

"I knew it," I respond with a slight and cheeky smile, humbly proud of myself. I am quite chuffed at myself for the level of will power I have used in order to arrive here. A part of me feels like the chosen human on earth but most of me, my heart, knows that this is a space for everyone. Everyone who chooses it.

"I would love to know who you are and why you are here with me at this moment? I mean, I know we are all connected to all time and space and can access all information but I don't know *exactly* who you are?" I ask.

She chuckles at me. "Well, Ostara, this space, this earthly heaven that we are in which is called Haven, is simply a space where you are out of your egoic mind enough to actually listen to a higher realm of information. Sometimes here in this space you need to ask questions to receive the answers rather than just knowing them as soon as you enter. The better the quality of your questions and the more specific you can be the more you will receive clear and direct information. So, since you have asked me who I am, I will answer you as clearly and directly as needed.

"My name is Sankai. I am one of your higher dimensional selves, one of your guardians. I have been with you from the moment you chose to be reborn into your earthly self and even eons before then. I have known you in many lifetimes in human form, celestial form and spirit form. My duty is to guide you through human life as human life is the most challenging to navigate as there are always dark forces who are willing to go to the ends of the earth to keep the light of the world dim.

They cast black magic on the sleeping to manipulate the people of the earth to forget to choose their own heart's expression. Although dark forces are not to be hated, they have simply forgotten their own heart's expression and believe they need to control and manipulate others so they can feel powerful again. There is much sadness in this as control and manipulation is an illusion of power and when you are in an illusion, you can never prevail. I am here with you Ostara, so you can be the remembrance for others around you, that you can always remain connected with love through every challenge, trial and tribulation. Love is forever present, floating in abundance and ready to be chosen the moment we all allow ourselves to feel, to truly feel to the depth of humanness. Hence why you have been on quite a journey of feeling in the time you have been through The Unconscious and Heart worlds. This is all intended for you to remember your own depth. Depth is what allows expansion within the higher realms," she says.

Huh, ok, that makes sense. Yet sounds totally crazy at the same time. I can feel the truth in it as clearly as I can feel the liquid against my body as I wade through water. Still I feel a sense of overwhelm. My purpose, this is my purpose. Well I guess this is the 'something more' that I was looking for.

"It will not be the end of the world if you do not choose your purpose here, Ostara. The world will not end because you don't choose to fulfill your service here to humanity by igniting their remembrance of true heart expression and the joy that comes with it. However, your heart will know, your soul will know and there are always consequences for not choosing your heart. No, you won't physically die, but your soul will to a degree and when your soul deteriorates your physical body deteriorates with it. If you just take a moment to look around at the world and notice how much physical pain is ever present. There are people with mental health issues, heart issues, back pain, kidney disease, dementia, alzheimers, the list goes on and on. Yes, there is a natural deterioration of the body as it ages, but life expectancy on earth is much, much higher than what science believes it to be. Two-hundred and fifty years is the true age of humans on earth to complete their life cycle. Humans are at far less than half of their life cycle before they pass. The secret, the golden ticket to the 250-year-old party is to stay connected here in the cosmic realm of the all-knowing which every human can access in any moment through intention, focus and the will to listen. When others have the will to connect here, they will always be connected to the golden thread of love even through all of the pain as the pain will no longer have the power. It will still exist but it won't have the power. In the presence of love and joy, all that is not that will come to the surface to be healed, and it will be healed at a rapid pace," she continues.

For a moment I allow myself to stop and receive the information. The overwhelm is real, yet the truth in it keeps me grounded in presence enough to receive the wisdom codes.

"So, I am one of the puzzle pieces for the reconnection to true heart. I am just one of the puzzle pieces that we all are in this world that needs to be expressed in a way of heart so we can all expand. Just for curiosity's sake, is this what happened to my Dad? He forgot his joy so therefore he forgot his own life? Or how to live a life in any sense of the heart?" I ask through my mind.

"Yes, that is correct. Your father has forgotten his soul as he believed that a part of his soul was with your mother and when she died, he chose to let a part of himself die with her. The part of him that he thought was no longer important was his will to create. He let his will die, his motivation and zest for life. Your mother was always very connected with me, with us in the cosmic realm and he always felt as though he was on the outside of that. He was never on the outside as we are always present in any given moment and if he had simply chosen to see his own power and greatness then we too would have been able to connect. When you were born, he let a part of himself die and he chose in that moment to simply get through life rather than to dance through life in harmony with his heart and soul. This is why you have always felt as though there was something more. You have always been very connected as through your whole gestation period your mother did many rituals, channelings and sought guidance from above and this was imprinted on you. Your whole life, until now, you have been wondering and yearning for the 'something more' in human life. That going to school, learning things that don't interest you, spending time with people who speak behind others backs, only to finish school and to find something you want to do for a job in a rush because what you desire is outside of the constructs of society's version of a 'normal' job, just isn't enough. This is why you have always felt out of sorts because you had always felt the magic of your own heart growing up, you always knew of the human capacity to create and to dream up your own life and this is why you had always felt like your father would never truly see you because he could never truly see his own joy and you were always a reflection of joy so he could never truly see you.

The truth is Ostara, humans are never simply humans. Inside every human is a magical creature that is yearning to be wild and free and the first step is noticing what is in the way of our freedom; our resistance per se, the second is finding a higher connection and choosing it, and the third is taking action," she says.

I feel the words culminating inside my mind. I can feel the thoughts swirling around my consciousness and cementing the information into the compartments within my brain. I see images, memories and visions that all relate to the very information that Sankai just delivered to me. The images, memories and visions allow me to remember the truth in the words that she speaks. I feel a sense of peace and calm come over my body and I realise something that has been holding me in a fear state for my whole life. I realise that it was not my fault that my mother died, it was not my doing that killed her, it was her purpose to leave. She was a puzzle piece in the bigger picture just like I am in mine. Her puzzle piece was complete and set. Her puzzle piece was perfectly woven into the very essence of who I am today. She imprinted me, she birthed me and guided me into leading her legacy into the future of my generation and thereafter.

A buzzing energy of vibrational love pours over my body and a tear of joy escapes my eye and drips onto the watery floor underneath my feet. The sound it makes, a drip that sings through the space like a singing bowl. I feel this sense of layers and layers of judgements and hatred towards myself melting off as my consciousness shifts under the light of the truth.

"There is freedom in truth," Sankai says as she is also experiencing what I am.

Her words are like a diamond in the sky, they radiate through me with grace and it is in this moment that I allow my truth to land in my being. It is as though I have stepped out of my own way and allowed my heart to sing. This is freedom. My whole life I always perceived freedom to be something you had to obtain, something you had to fight for, or something only people who were rich would choose.

Freedom is the truth and following the truth of your heart's calling. Arghhh I get it! I squeal to myself internally. I get it. I feel like I have just won the golden ticket to the Willy Wonka chocolate factory but the chocolate factory is the joy factory. I guess you could say chocolate and joy are the same thing. They are to me anyway.

Sankai smiles at me and my thoughts.

"It is so nice hanging out with you Sankai, it is really nice being here and spending this time or what actually seems to be timelessness with you. I feel like I could live here forever and experience a whole entire lifetime in a moment of my normal human time," I say.

"You are right, Ostara. You can do that. You can experience many shifts, experiences, wisdoms, love or whatever you need to experience here in a very quick time. Time only exists for human minds to orient themselves. Here, in this higher space, you can collect any information you need to collect for your visions, your next steps and where you are needing to change in order to move forward. All you need to do is to remember that we are here, I am here. Have the intention to slow down, breathe and connect and you will hear me, see me and feel me," she replies.

"I can do that. I have only just recently learned how great deep breathing feels. I have no idea how I left it so long to learn that. How was I breathing before? Obviously very shallowly. I guess that it is a red flag for when I am not in my heart right?"

Sankai nods with pride.

"What are my next steps? I ask.

"First step, reconnect with your mother. She is here, all you need to do is call on her and she will come. Reconnecting with your mother is supportive of you moving forward and knowing she never really left you. She was always around you in spirit."

I feel a hint of nervousness but it is only a flavour of it. Above the nervousness is mostly excitement. Excitement that I no longer need to feel heaviness when I think about her. Ok Ostara, call upon your mother. I think to myself. All I need to do is think about her.

I close my eyes and picture her in front of me, come to me Mum. I whisper to myself. I wish to reconnect with you. I take the deepest and longest breath in an out with a sigh and then I open my eyes with hope of seeing mum.

Chapter Fifteen

The Reconnection

She sparkles just like the stars behind her as she floats closely to Sankai. She wears a black robe with what looks like a golden language weaved through it that meets the floor. They look at each other like they are long-time friends who are reuniting, resurrected as new beings. There is wonder in their eyes, and curiousness in their energy almost a childlike innocence. Erotic and delightful, yet powerful and trusting. The stars will forever remind me of all the souls who knew it was their time to return home, they will always remind me of my mother.

She is just there floating like an angel and smiling at me with eyes that hold pride, so much pride that if she had tears, she would cry. I assume that spirits don't cry but for some reason I can. I feel a tear escape my eye again. I don't think I have ever cried out of pure joy so much in all my life. Nope. Never. This Haven place is truly magical. This remembrance of worlds far out of my own is what I have been dreaming of my entire life.

I hear her voice reverberate through my mind as if she was speaking to me out loud.

"I am so proud of everything you have achieved in your life, Ostara. All the trials and tribulations, hardships and heartbreak you have handled with grace and softness as you learn along the way. You truly have lived on, in a way that I had always dreamed of. I am so thankful you listened to my dreams and yours," she says.

Words escape me. I don't know what to say but smile as tears pour down my cheeks. I have waited all my life for someone to reassure me of my path, to reassure me that I am loved, wholly.

She opens her arms to invite me in for a hug. I run. Except running in this space is not really running, it is more like floating or gliding across the watery floor. I float into her arms and to my surprise it feels human-like. I never expected her to feel like this as she looks *sooo* spirit-like. Then I remember that I am in a place of magic, so anything is possible if you intend it. I melt. With every breath I take I breathe more of her in, I breathe in her essence with the intention of holding her within my being after I leave Haven. Memories flood my mind again as I dip back into my last memories of feeling this close to her. Tears are pouring from my eyes now as I re-experience all of the memories of her as a babe so new to human form, all the memories I had forgotten. She says nothing. Just holds me in love. I feel it. I feel all of it. All of her love, her compassion, her kindness, her essence. I feel her sadness as she had to leave me so young and I also feel her certainty in the truth of it. I feel it all. The strange part for my mind to process is how much joy I feel in feeling it all. Like a golden thread is always connected to the essence of truth through all the emotion. It is peaceful and I melt even deeper.

She whispers in my mind, "This is your gift for the world baby, gift the world with the golden thread of waking dreams. Show them how to find their golden thread of heart. This is the something more you have been looking for," she says.

I nod, still nuzzled in her sparkly arms.

"I promise. I will live out my purpose, Mum, I promise I will never let my heart down. I will choose it until it is the last thing I do as a human," I say.

Love vibrates through my body and ripples out into the cosmic world through my mother and through Sankai. A pulse of light shoots through my body.

Suddenly a million memories comes back into my mind. I remember the black and golden robe my mother is wearing. I remember Maiden, I remember the being from the forest in which I fell who wore the same robe. I remember… The moment when Maiden told me I had to forget her and one day I would understand. I remember the sadness I felt when she told me so. I remember…. Mum has been here all along just in a different form.

"You remember now, and with this remembering you have your powers back. You had to forget for a time in order for you to live a normal teenage life. If you had all of your powers through your teenage years it would have created so much pain. Under the spiritual laws in which we are governed all magic children must go through a period of separation from their powers in order to learn to be a 'normal' human. When the child is ready, they will go through an initiation journey, as you now have, so they too can remember. There are many others like you Star, waiting to meet you, when you're ready to help us in their world.

Tears flood my eyes as pieces of my life finally fall into place. Where I had felt huge gaps in my life, start to fill with understanding and compassion. Gratitude fills my eyes and relief encompasses me as I let all that I had forgotten drip into every crevice of my mind so I never forget again. Every word my mother has spoken has filled in the gaps that I had always

107

perceived to be a curse. It all makes so much sense. A sense that doesn't make sense in earth laws but sense in magic.

More tears of humble joy flow from my whelming eyes as I feel all of the puzzle pieces of me fall into place and I feel the deepest sense of my true self take residence in my being forever. Never to be lost again.

With that, I feel a sense of completion. Like I have been playing a video game and have completed the highest level. Now I get to move onto the next game. This sense of completion feels like an initiation into a new way of living, a new way of being, a new way for the whole world, not just me. I feel as though I have completed the third step through a spectrum of emotions, through a spectrum of colours, flavours and experiences. Completeness brings a new sense of pleasure. This time, the pleasure is embodied. A full body experience. Not just an experience of sensual pleasure or hearty pleasure. It's a full body pleasure. I mean, I feel it in my toes and fingertips. Everything buzzes like my cells are dancing with each other in romance. I feel this sense of completion but the completion simply feels as though it is a beginning, like some kind of magical rebirthing and in that rebirthing I have grown an insatiable appetite for life, for momentum, for hearty action. My stomach feels solid yet fluid at the same time, my heart is open and its consciousness is awakened to purpose. Nothing feels more potent than this knowing of the journey only starting. My vision is clear, my faith is renewed and I trust my actions to come in the moment. Trust. A word I would never have used in the past. But here I trust, wholeheartedly and faithfully in the experience of coming home to feeling like me, all of me.

I gently let go of my mother as I come into the reclamation of my truth, like a ready warrior for the battle to come. The battle of my purpose.

I look her in the eyes as they sparkle against the light of the stars in the sky. She nods with a smile. "You *are* ready," she internally communicates to me. "One last thing," she says.

She reaches down to my hand and points to her ring that I have on my finger. The last two stones have reached their capacity of light and they shine so brightly with a beautiful purple colour and pure white light. I could stare at these stones for days and totally forget about the time.

"This ring will always be a reminder of your home." She taps my chest, my stomach and my temples. "This will always be a reminder of your true nature and purpose here on earth, your true calling in life. If you ever get lost, ask for guidance and it will show you the way. And remember, all you need is to trust in your golden thread. Follow that thread and you will find your way," she says.

"I will Mum. I promise. I've got this," I say and I puff out my chest as I embody a warrior-like energy.

I turn my head to Sankai and bow in thanks to her wisdom.

"Thank you for your guidance. I promise to keep listening. I promise to stay connected."

"I have no doubt in you Ostara, it has been an honour as always," she replies. "Though, you can't go just yet as I have a gift for you. You have made it through to a new level of awareness and you will need greater strengths for what is coming, in your earth world and other worlds. You will need great strength as one day you will need to fight for what is true. You won't need to fight in a way that you might know it now but in other ways.

"You will need your heart weapon. Every human has heart weapons but they don't know it. Everyone has a weapon of the heart that they can use in higher dimension spaces and lower dimensional spaces that hold specific gifts. You my dear, have the sacred Emerald torch," she says, pulling a staff like torch out of thin air in front of my eyes.

It is holographic green with intricate golden features weaved through it like veins. The handle is silver white and has green emeralds on the top of it to take centre stage of glory that shine like a torch. I instantly connect intimate with it as it feels familiar, known, like I am meant to have this in my life. I smile as I feel the essence of it, of me in it.

"This is not like a torch as most on earth would believe. You can use her when you are needing direction as she will work like a compass to show you the way, she will light up so bright as you choose the truth, and will flicker in colour when there is danger around. She will help your will, strengthen your love and compassion and she will keep all of your chakras centres in alignment. And, when you really learn to connect with her, you will be able to charge them to teleport to wherever you need to go. I say she as her name is Ikshana. There are many uses for this gift, Ostara and you will learn over time, but for now, simply receive her and allow her to start working through you at her own pace. Don't rush it as it will be too much for your energy, simply let it all unfold. You will need her in the future, so for now, let her be what she is to you and more will reveal itself," says Sankai.

She ushers the Ikshana torch over to me without moving herself. It simply floats towards me and I take a deep breath into my uncertainty of what will happen next. The torch gently enters my heart and a shot of energy runs through my body and I gasp at the intensity of the feeling. Heat rushes through every cell and oxygen pumps through my heart. I pant in response like I have just run a marathon. I hear whispers of a thousand voices echoing through my mind, like a thousand souls live in this emerald all wishing to tell me a story at the same time. I can't isolate a single voice to make out what they are saying, but I know that what they are saying isn't necessary for me to know right now, but I will over time. I remember to keep breathing, to keep allowing and eventually the whispers get quieter and my mind falls into stillness again. My body feels new and my mind is the quietest it has ever been. I feel whole. Just whole and in peace as the last piece of me comes home.

I take some deep breaths and look around, taking a moment to revel in the beauty of this heavenly place. Everything looks so magical here. Magic is real. Magic is everything and we are a speck of it, but all of it.

"It is time for you to go home my love. It is time for you to return to Billie and your father. Your father will come around once he sees how you have changed in life and the changes you will make, he will learn from you. Just be in your essence and he will follow. I am so proud of you Ostara, I love you so much," Mum says.

My heart feels like it has exploded in my chest. It is almost too much to handle but everything I have ever wanted.

"I love you too mum. I love you so *so* much," I say with tears in my eyes. Then I hear the thought arise in my mind. But how do I get home?

My ring finger buzzes and rainbow colours engulf my body. The last thing I see is my mother blowing me a kiss and the heavenly world of Haven melts away.

Chapter Sixteen

The Integration

All that is familiar to me at this moment is my breath, it is my anchor. My breath is my anchor into some sort of reality. The more I breathe, the more deeply I am starting to feel human again. With every breath I take I slowly start to feel my physical human form again, rather than being an energy that is somewhere unhuman, I am starting to feel the gravity that is holding me to this earth, I am starting to feel my organs and the feeling is becoming visceral now. My ears are ringing with a celestial sound, yet with every breath the sound becomes a hum and the hum becomes the sound of the trees. What I once heard as a muffled sound is now clear to me that it is the voice of Billie. A familiarity, a sound of home, a sound of reality. I feel a slight smile on my face, yet I have no idea why I am smiling or what I am smiling about. It is just happening and it feels more natural to me than ever before. I start to feel my fingers, my toes wiggle and I notice that my hands are placed firmly on the ground in front of me. I slowly open my eyes to look at the grass underneath my hands and I feel overjoyed with the sensations pulsating through me from the earth, it excites me. I don't think I have ever been so overjoyed with grass before. It is as though I am seeing it for the first time through infant eyes, through a new lens of wonder, curiosity and excitement. As I stare at the grass, the blades gently dance in the wind, like every blade of grass has its own little personality and I am seeing each and every one of them express themselves through their response to the wind. It is as though they are putting on a performance for me. I giggle in response. Nothing else around me has my attention. I am totally infatuated and present with my connection to the earth, I can viscerally feel its magic, it's heartbeat. I can feel the earth breathing through me like I am simply a vessel for her expression. All I have just experienced is becoming tangible, something I can now feel in my reality.

I can feel Billie's presence, I can feel his eyes on me in wonder like I have somewhat lost it, yet he knows I am ok from the giggle I let out. He has always been great like that. He has always been in tune with me to some degree and never overly worried about me in any sense. He has always had a deep trust in me and I never really understood why but now I have returned from an entire internal journey I can understand why, I can understand what he felt in me. I can now feel it myself. I feel a buzz in my pocket and I remember my mother's ring. I giggle again as I realise how I just experienced an entire world totally out of this physical world as the ring is no longer on my finger. The ring is exactly where I had left it when I first found it. My mind is both blown yet totally at peace. In unity. It all feels so true, it all feels so humbling and nourishing. Like a battle has taken place and I can now move on to bigger and more advanced ways of living.

I take a moment to give thanks to myself, to the journey, to the experiences I just received and to the earth for holding me here right now, now is all I can perceive... in a moment of devotion to myself and to the magic of living. I feel overwhelmed with joy in the simplicity of it all. Another giggle escapes my throat again and my ears finally start listening to Billie this time.

"Ostara, can you tell me what is going on? I have heard you giggle three times now and I would love it if you would tell me what is going on? Are you ok? Or are you not ok? Are you somewhere else? Do I need to be concerned?" he asks in a direct manner.

I take a deep breath with a smile on my face and I look up at him sitting in front of me with a puzzled look on his face like a confused puppy.

He is so beautiful. The energy around him swirls. I can see it like you can see leaves caught in a willy-willy. His energy sparkles, the kind of sparkles that kids would love to paint with. I take him in, in full appreciation for a boy with a heart of gold. I breathe him in for a moment, I breath in his sparkles and the essence of his greatness before I speak.

"I am better than ever Billie. I am more than ok," I reply with the energy of joy weaved through my words.

He sighs and screws up his face at my words like they licked him in the face. I can see how desperately he wants an explanation from me.

"Right, I am glad you are ok Ostara, but I would love to know what just happened? You went all weird and then fell asleep. I mean it's pretty normal for you to be weird at times, I guess that's one of the things I love most about you, but this was a different kind of weird, like you had no idea what reality was for a moment. Then you went silent for five minutes. You didn't reply to anything I said, you just lay there breathing really deeply like you suddenly went into the deepest meditation or something. So don't mind me, I am just a little curious as to what happened," he says sarcastically.

I giggle again and he huffs in response. He is so cute when he is annoyed.

"If I tell you, will you promise to not call me crazy?" I ask.

"When have I ever called you crazy? I mean aren't we all? Yeah, I may have called you crazy in the past but I have always meant it as a term of endearment, ya know? Like friends do."

"Ok buckle up princess, you are in for a ride," I reply. As the words escape my mouth I remember that those words were the words I had heard before I got sucked into a portal and into a different reality. I feel like I have gone a full circle but this time I don't feel heavy, I feel totally free and excited to share.

"Right I suppose I will get comfy then," Billie says and shuffles in his seat to sit upright. He nods at me as if to give me permission to start speaking.

I take a deep breath and start to explain to Billie every detail of my experience. I go into the details of all the sensations I had in my body leading up to entering the portal. I tell him everything about Helvac, everything about my child self, my mother, Sankai and the ring. As I explain every detail, I closely observe his facial expressions. Some tell me he is excited by the story and others tell me he is questioning my sanity, yet none of it bothers me. It feels important to share it with him as he has always been my side kick, my best bud and confidant. Sharing such a transformative experience out loud allows it all to start to feel somewhat normal.

As I reach the end of sharing my experience of my time in the cosmos with Sankai and my mother I see a sadness come over his face. A sadness that tells me he wishes he had an experience like that, that he could have had such a time in a place that seemed so out of this world. There is sadness in his eyes, yet I still feel his unwavering support through him listening to me and giving me presence throughout.

My hands are dancing around as I attempt to reenact the movements of my body so he can receive a visual experience as well as the explanation through words.

After twenty minutes of me speaking and him listening, I take a deep breath and complete my story.

"And then, I heard your voice that brought me back here right now. And here I am, the same, yet totally different. Like I am the same person with the same life, with the same family, the same past, yet my outlook on life is completely different. Like the lens I am seeing through is new like a kaleidoscope of magic," I say with excitement.

I meet his gaze as I complete my story and I wait. I wait for a response. For the first time in our entire friendship, he has nothing to say. He just blinks at me, still computing the information I just gave him. I feel a moment of fear as I hear a thought come into my mind that says, 'what if he rejects me and calls me crazy'. I take a moment to acknowledge the thought and let it go as I choose to see Billie in his greatness as he receives such wild and new information. He is silent for what feels like an eternity.

"You did all of that in five minutes?" he finally asks.

I sigh in relief that words came out of his mouth.

"Yes," is all I can manage to get out. Yet I say it with such certainty that he nods in response. He nods with curiosity and wonder and in that moment, I know that he is supportive of my experiences. He gets it. He doesn't fully understand but he believes me.

"Do you think you could do it all again? I mean, do you think this is something you can control or it just happens to you?" he asks.

Great question I think to myself.

"This time around, I didn't have control over it. It just happened to me but I know now that it was necessary for it to happen so unexpectedly so I could realise that I can access any of these spaces at any time. It might take some practice but I have unwavering faith in myself that I can do it again. I also know that I will be able to teach it if I need to," I reply.

His eyes light up like an excited puppy that sees food coming around the corner.

"I would love to know how you did that. It would be cool to be on the same wavelength with you and experience that for myself. It seems like you had a lot of healing there and this makes me happy to hear," he says with softness in his voice.

My heart palpitates in response to the love and support I feel from him. I meet his eyes with love and thanks.

"Thank you, Billie. It always warms my heart to feel how supportive you are of me in life. You are such a special friend to me," I say with tenderness in my voice.

He smiles in response.

I roll onto my back and throw my arms out the side to melt into the grass and I sigh as my head hits the earth. I gesture for Billie to lie down too. He does, as he is still computing all the information and trying to make sense of it.

"There is no need to make sense of it all Billie. It was an experience that initiated me more deeply into myself and that's all that needs to be made sense of," I say. I even surprise myself at the wisdom that comes out of my mouth. Like I have suddenly become a modern day Yoda.

"Do you think you could teach me how to do the same thing so I can be more confident in speaking to Melina?" He asks.

I had almost forgotten why we had come out to the magical paddock in the first place; to practice the 'asking Melina out' conversation.

"Well Billie, my first thought is that you don't need to find the confidence to speak to Melina. There isn't anything to find because it is already there. You have everything you need without me to ask her. All you need to do is be honest and vulnerable about how you feel. When you speak from the heart it will be reciprocated, it's the law of one."

"Since when did you become Yoda? Is that what the cosmos taught you? To become Yoda?" he says.

My thoughts exactly I think to myself as I giggle at his response.

"That is all and well, I understand what you mean but what do I need to do to not be so scared of it?" he asks.

"What is it about Melina that brings you joy? What is it that you love about her or your interactions?" I ask.

"Well, I hadn't thought of that before. That's a good question. It also feels like this is an adult Ostara question. Let me just think for a minute," says Billie.

"No don't think, just feel," I reply.

He gives me a slight look as the words that escaped my mouth were words that he hadn't heard from me before and to be honest I hadn't heard them come out of my mouth before either. This really is a big change in me and I know he can see it too. I notice him close his eyes and then tilt his head to the side.

"How do I do that? How do I... feel things? I mean I know that we can all feel emotions but is it like a sensation or is it something else?" he asks.

"Well, it can be both. Sometimes there may be heat in your belly if you are angry, sometimes you might feel butterflies in your stomach if you are anxious, sometimes you might feel heaviness in your heart if there is grief there, sometimes you might feel a warmth in your lower belly if you feel aroused. Sometimes you feel it tangibly and other times you feel it more subtly. I have only just discovered this myself. I didn't know how to feel things before either, but I guess I was shown how to feel for a reason, to teach it to others who want to remember how to feel the joy of their hearts and the whole spectrum of the possibilities there," I say.

"Hmmm," Billie responds.

I can hear his mind ticking a hundred miles an hour trying to work out what I mean logically.

"Thinking logically doesn't work Billie. Close your eyes and let me see if I can help you. I can only try," I say.

He nods at me with a concerned look on his face, yet he closes his eyes in trust of me.

"Now, simply take a few deep breaths right into your belly. Let your belly expand like a big balloon and when you breathe out let it be lengthy, longer than your in-breath. Now imagine yourself to be in the presence of Melina and watch how she moves, how she does life, how she is as a person, let yourself breathe her in," I explain. I pause and give him a moment.

"Now, ask yourself, what brings you joy about Melina? What sensations do you feel in your body and where do you feel them? And, trust whatever comes to your mind first. Trust the first thing that pops into your head after I ask you that question and just start speaking whenever you have received some information," I continue to explain.

I pause again and witness him, as I can see his imagination going wild. I can see his eyes darting back and forth as he is watching Melina dance in his imagination. I am in awe of his ability to stay here with me in the newness of me that he hasn't experienced before. I am in awe that he is not running away from me like my fear assumed he would. He is a solid human and I can see that now more than ever before. A true friend. A true companion. It is almost as though he has never doubted my essence as he signed a contract to be my soul explorer in the world. My sidekick that never faulted in seeing my greatness. I am sure my mother sent him here to guide me through life. I mean, after all I have so recently experienced I know that all things are divinely placed.

"Aha! I get it. Oh boy I can feel it in my loins!" Billie squeals and he grabs his man treasure like it holds precious stones.

I can't help but burst out laughing. "We have made it!" I say through the bursts of laughter.

Billie has opened his eyes now and he is also laughing with me. He pats me on the knee multiple times to get my attention as he laughs with me. "Ok ok can I tell you now? I want to tell you what I feel. I am proud of myself for feeling anything at all. How cool! And how easy is that… like I was looking for something complicated and mind breaking but it's really simple," he says.

He really has got it. He is remembering. So quickly and gracefully, he is remembering.

"Yes, you are simply remembering Billie. You are remembering your innate abilities. Go on, tell me all the things. I would love to hear it," I say.

"At first I didn't think I felt anything but the more I thought about her pretty face and the way her pony tail swings from side to side as she walks and the way one side of her lip curls when she is deep in thought when I am saying something left field. Then I started to feel a little flutter in my chest, like a love feeling I am guessing. AND THEN! I started to feel some movement downstairs. Ya know, like that lil guy is starting to wake up but not wake up. Like it's not the little guy it's his two mates that are just starting to heat up. It was cool, I hadn't really felt that before. Or maybe I was just never aware of it. I guess this is the feeling that drives people to make babies huh," he says with a smirk.

"Fabulous! So. In saying all of that. What brings you joy about Melina?"

"She is so smart, she laughs at my jokes, she is so free in being herself, she is curious and likes to learn things and I can see that she is a little weird like we are. I want to know more of that weirdness ya know?" he says.

As he says these words my own heart feels lit up at the feeling of him expressing his love in a way that is true for him.

"And that, my friend, is all you need to say," I reply with a loving smile on my face as I poke him in the heart.

"See all you need to do is listen to what brings you joy, listen to your heart in each moment and the right thing will come. I mean I am not going to claim to be a guru but what I will claim is that this is what I learnt in the weird and wonderful experience I just had. And the doubts. The doubts that you have will always be there but we have a choice to act from the doubt or action, regardless of the doubt, out of love and joy. And that's all I need to say. I don't need to pretend to be you, I don't need to put the words in your mouth. You have it already to speak, it just needs to be spoken."

Billie looks a little defeated but not in a bad way. In a way of acceptance, like he is letting go of what he thought he wanted it to be and letting it be what it already is. I patiently wait for a reply, simply holding time and space while his mind ticks over.

"Yeah, I guess you're right. That isn't what I want to hear though. What I want to hear is that I don't have to do it, that someone else will take over my body while I speak so I can hide while it's all happening. I know, I know, I can't do that but a part of me wants to."

I giggle again as I can totally relate to wanting this in the past. I have flashes of memories in my mind of wanting to speak to boys I have had crushes on and never did it. All those times when I hadn't spoken from my heart in fear of it being rejected. Things feel so different now. Everything feels more... Simple.

"What's the worst thing that will happen? She rejects you, doesn't want to date you and then what?" I ask.

"Umm... I will be totally embarrassed for the rest of my life!" he yells.

"You won't die though. You might be embarrassed for a while, you might be sad, you might feel shit about it but you won't die. You will still be breathing. You will still be alive. It doesn't mean anything about you," I reply with an element of playful mockery running through my voice.

"And," I continue, "You will still be loved. You will still have me, you will still have your family, your knowledge, the trees around you, all of your other friends, your football mates, a home, you will still be able to eat food, travel, sleep, breathe. All the things you need. You will still have it all even if you don't get the girl. AND what is to say that you won't? I mean, what girl would want to reject or shame someone who is speaking from their heart? If you truly see all of those beautiful things in her and you speak from that place of truth then she will receive it one way or another. Ya feeling me?"

Billie's cheeks go red. He looks like he got caught red handed masturbating for the first time. I can feel that the embarrassment comes from knowing the discomfort that will come from the conversation. Not that the realisation was embarrassing for him, but at the thought of the possible embarrassment. I continue to speak as I can feel the tension in him about to pop as he realises and remembers his own power in choice.

"Would you rather live your life by what embarrassing thing might possibly happen, or live your life by assuming the best possible outcome and going for that?" I ask. The words coming out of my mouth seem as though someone else is saying them and I am simply a vessel. It is a strange feeling to be shocked by my own words of wisdom that I had never thought were in there either. I can almost feel Billie going through the same realisation. The joy it brings me to see him unfolding is second to none. How did I ever live my life before? I am not sure, but I like this new me and almost new Billie.

To my shock and surprise Billie jumps to his feet and assumes a warrior stance with his fists on his hips, his chest puffed out and a determined look on his face. Yup, there you have it. He has popped out the other side of his fear. That didn't take long. He is a trooper!

"Right! I feel nervous, but I am ready. I am so ready. To pour my heart out, to claim my lady and to claim myself in the process. I am nervous as fuck but you are right, Ostara, how can I live my life by all the bad things that might happen? I ain't about that. I am about fun. Life is fun so I've gotta act like that. Even when it scares the shit out of me. I'm ready. I'm ready. I'm ready," he says, as he nods his head and folds his arms in ownership of what he has announced. He looks like he is getting ready for battle.

I start clapping. I have absolutely no idea why I am clapping but my assumption is that a clap is what he needs for that extra little kick up in his confidence.

"Well Billie, confidence was your intention for this evening. So? Do you feel like you have achieved that?" I ask while I am *still* clapping.

"Fuck yeah! I mean, maybe I am all fired up now after our conversation but something in the words that you spoke snapped me out of it. It's like I was a different human when I was scared of it. Now I feel a little stupid for even thinking that way. I mean, maybe I will forget this confidence tomorrow but what I can do is resume this stance and remember today. That might work. I can only give it a red-hot crack," he says with such passion in his voice.

"Fuck yeah!" I squeal as I jump to my feet and fist pump.

If anyone was filming us right now you would think we were auditioning for The Vikings to be central characters in a battle scene. We are fist pumping, jumping up and down and I am sure that if any famous performer witnessed us they would one-hundred percent hire us to be their hype girl and guy. What a time it is to be alive. I think to myself. I have a moment of emotion wash over me. A moment of pure joy and love in what has simply unfolded through our conversation. To see Billie shift in such brief moments and for him to remember his own confidence and greatness so quickly. I feel emotion at how much pressure from life has just melted off me simply by letting go of how it is, or how I think it needs to be. I feel emotion in how much joy and love I feel in my heart in the smallest of moments. I am simply here with my best friend, jumping up and down, laughing and fist pumping. It is the smallest moment in the scheme of life. This concept really is landing in my heart of hearts.

"I love you Billie and I am so grateful to have you in my life. You are a true friend and I couldn't think of anyone better to spend most of my time with," I glee with a hearty smile on my face.

He immediately stops and looks slightly shocked, but more so wanting to be present for me as I speak vulnerably.

He sighs a deep sigh. "This is the first time I have really felt like you have meant the words 'I love you' Ostara. I love you too. I'm still not sure of what the hell happened to you in your other world only moments ago but whatever you experienced has made a difference. You are pretty spesh to me too," he says while he fist bumps my shoulder.

I can't help but smile in response, a little shy.

"I am curious to see how things will be different with you and your dad. I know that relationship has always been a challenge for you so I am intrigued to see how you go," he adds.

I feel a little pang in my belly. A pang of nervousness. How will I respond to my dad? I know I have never projected at him or had a bad relationship with him but there was always an element of sadness there. Like I had convinced myself that he hated me because I was the one who killed my mother. There is a pang of nervousness; yet woven through the nervousness is curiosity. I am excited to see how I respond, like I am entering into a new phase and it is a challenge that I can conquer.

"You know what, I am excited. Nervous-excited. Like I am about to embark on a new journey with him. One that is more heart-centred than it has been for a long time. But. I guess we will find out, hey," I say as I swing my arm across my body in eager readiness.

"Yeah, I guess we will. Shall we?" Billie gestures towards the house.

"Yeah, let's do it," I say with a flavour of nervousness in my voice.

Billie smiles at me, throws his arm around me and we set off towards home. Never have I felt so supported. Never have I felt so ready to take on whatever life throws at me.

Chapter Seventeen

Infant Eyes

This pulsing. This new layer of being. This new layer of feeling is all I can focus on. I am sitting on my bed in a position that might look like a yogi, like a meditation position and with my index and middle finger I am tapping my chest. It feels so nice and I can see in my imagination that my heart is pulsing out energy in the same pattern as you would see when you throw a stone into water and the water ripples out for ages. This is exactly what I am seeing in my mind's eye. My heart feels like it is opening and softening with every tap and I am enjoying the process. This new layer of being me is so new, it feels like I am born again, discovering who I am all over again, yet from the perspective of awe and wonder, like a child. I feel as though, with every tap, there is a layer of clearing, like the tapping is moving something through me like a cat when it purrs to communicate how content it is. It is like each tap is doing just that.

As I tap my chest I reflect on the day and what a rollercoaster it was for me. It is late at night now and I could claim to have lived a whole lifetime in one day. Is that even possible? It feels true to me so I guess that is all that matters.

My palms feel sweaty and I feel tingling right in the centre of them. The tingling is so tangible that I must play with it like I played in multiple realms today. It all feels like such a fun exploration of a new world. My palms tingle and I hear the words, "bring them together and feel" and I know that it is Sankai communicating with me from behind the veil of other worlds. Her voice relaxes my body in knowing that what I had experienced today wasn't all just made up in my head, because it continues. There are moments of doubt in my mind when I think back through today's memories, it all feels so unreal that my mind wants to convince me it wasn't real. Yet, I still hear Sankai's voice like she is in the room with me and her voice grounds me back into what is tangibly real.

I bring my hands in front of my chest, palms about a centimetre apart, take some deep breaths and set my focus upon feeling. The tingling in my hands gets stronger and I feel a force, like when you put two magnets together on their opposing sides, how they resist each other. It feels like I am wading my hands through water to bring my hands together to meet. I pull them outwards again and feel a magnetic force wanting to keep my hands together. I imagine that if I could tangibly see the force between my hands it would be like an energy ball that buzzes and pops and twirls around, like *dragon ball-z*.

I could sit here forever and play with this energy, it is so much fun. My heart feels so full and satisfied with right here and right now and all I am doing is spending time with my own energy. This is what the yogi's always talk about, this is what the ancient spiritual teachers are always trying to teach about presence, the right here and right now. I finally get it.

It has landed and made its way home into my heart. It's the small things in life. The magic of feeling, of resonating with your own energy field. It's the most home I will ever feel.

A giggle escapes my chest. I can't help it. I don't even know why I feel so much joy, I just do. It's a moment that can only be shared by me and a moment that I have to be in the here and now to fully appreciate. It cannot be repeated.

I remember my grandad-father and how he always said he had magical hands that could feel and heal, and that it was not just him who had magical hands but we all do. All humans on earth have the ability to feel what is intangible in a tangible world. His words of wisdom come flooding back to me as I continue to play with the new energy game I have found.

Tears of joy start to stream down my face as I am taken over by total awe. I don't think I have ever cried so much in all my life, not tears of joy, that was never a thing for me but now it is and I really like it. I cry at the thought of feeling magic so tangibly in between my hands. And really feeling it. I always knew that healers could feel things but I never knew how and never thought that I could ever feel things to this degree. What a gift it is to be human. After all these years believing I was a curse in the world for being here, for always thinking I was the reason my mother left this earth and hated myself for it. There is a teaspoon of truth in it, I was one of the reasons my mother left this earth but it was her choice, it was a part of her soul contract here on earth when she decided to come here.

Now more than ever, I feel closer to her. Dad always said she was a wise, spiritual woman and I never really understood spirituality until now. It is simply feeling the subtleties of life that are always there, just hidden behind a veil that is so thin, anyone can access it. Simply but not easily.

I can't wait to see how this new me will impact others around me. I don't feel like I am ready to teach others yet, not by a long shot, but I am willing to see how this will help my dad.

Oh Dad, you are my biggest challenge.

"He is the starting point, so much healing starts with family as most trauma happens in childhood," I hear Sankai whisper in my ear.

"I agree. But did you see how he responded today?" I reply with frustration in my voice.

"Yes. But did you see how differently he responded to how he normally does?"

"Yeah, I guess so" I can feel the tension in my stomach as I have a desire to connect with him again.

"Today was progressive. Now get some sleep as there is much more to come," says Sankai

Chapter Eighteen

Earlier today - The test

One foot in front of the other. The anticipation feels like water around my body and I am wading through it. Everything is almost in slow motion as I take each step closer and closer to home. I feel nervous about how I will respond to Dad. I have spent years feeling so disconnected from him, like I never really had a father at all and I have always felt so desperate to reconnect. The nervousness comes from the desire to be held with love by him, to be held and seen as a young woman who wants a relationship with her father. There is excitement in my heart as I feel a sense of expansion coming, like an instrumental in a song, it's the anticipated finale.

I start to pep talk myself, follow the golden thread, I think to myself. That is all I need to remind myself, to follow the golden thread. Underneath and intertwined with it all is always love. Love is the very essence of life itself. See him in his greatness. Be vulnerable. Keep your heart open. Stay grounded.

"What ya thinking?" I am whipped out of my deep pep talk by Billie's voice.

I look at him strangely like he has just told me he wet his pants on the walk over. I forgot for a moment that I was walking beside Billie as I had been so deep in my own mind.

"I am feeling ready, ready to test this new perspective of mine, or way of being I should say," I say with a cheeky smile.

Billie responds with a shoulder bump and a nod like we are two bad-asses going to run amuck.

I feel excited to step through the door and give my dad a hug, but not just any hug, a hug that says, I love you. A hug that says you are powerful, you're great. A hug that says I will love you no matter what. A hug that assures him that the world is a beautiful place to be. A hug that allows him to remember his own joy that is locked away in his chest. I have the vision of this hug replaying over and over in my mind and I get the feelings, sensations and emotions that come with it. I can really *feel* the moment it happens. The more I feel the hug, the more powerful and quick my steps become, like I am marching into battle to show how ready I am for this.

"Look him in the eye, Ostara, keep your eyes with him." I hear Sankai whisper in my ear.

Got it. I think to myself. I can do that. I open the door like Dora the Explorer arriving home from a big day out with Patrick collecting adventures.

"Hey love. Hey Billie" Dad says with a forced hearty expression. "That was quite an entry," he continues.

My heart starts to beat a little faster in anticipation for my next moves. I don't even know what my next moves are, as I am not meant to. I am waiting for a limb to move, or something to move. My feet aren't quite ready to move forward yet and I am ok with that. I am still catching up after such anticipation.

"Can ya move please? I'm kinda stuck in the doorway," Billie says in a half whisper.

"Oh, oops, sorry Billie," I say as I step aside. Now I am a little nervous and unsure about myself. It wasn't what I was expecting. I don't even know what I was expecting. Some sort of a movie scene. I can be dramatic like that. It's just my dad for God's sake. Chill out Ostara.

"What have you kids been up to? Apart from cross dressing." Dad's voice snaps me back into reality.

"Oh uhmmm, well," I remember that I am wearing trackie pants, boots, a t-shirt that is oversized for such a small frame and a farmer's hat. I giggle out loud at the remembrance of what I am wearing. The giggle continues and I can't even stop it. I keep laughing at myself as I remember how ridiculous I look and I love the fact that my own ridiculousness can diffuse the tension I am feeling. A part of me that I was once so awkward about.

The giggle turns into a cackle and the cackle is so ridiculous that now it's the thing that is making me laugh and of course I can hear Billie's bellowing laugh in the background of my cackles. I laugh so much that tears are running down my face and I crumple over as my stomach starts to ache from all of the joy. Even with this amount of joy you still experience the discomfort of laughing pains. What a poetic metaphor for life.

I haven't even thought to look at my dad yet because I am too immersed in my own laughing fit. Perhaps this is all to avoid experiencing my dad in a new way. I don't care though, I simply let the laughing fit ride its way out and enjoy every moment of it.

"Damn, laughing is painful," I say as I try to catch my breath. "And I have no idea why that was so funny, it just was," I continue.

"What have you done with my daughter? This girl is a giggle pot," Dad says.

I instantly feel myself get offended and I feel a heat in the pit of my stomach. How dare he try and squish my joy! I think to myself. Shouldn't he be happy for me that I am happy? Why does he need to question who I am because I am happy? Just because he is always miserable, doesn't mean everyone else needs to be. God damn it! Now I am in my head. Fuck. Now the silence has been too long. Fuck. What a rollercoaster the last five minutes has been. More like two hours I should say. Fuck.

'Just take a breath, Ostara. Remember your heart and his greatness not his pain,' I hear Sankai say.

I instantly respond with a deep breath. Oh yes. I forgot how grounding breathing is. Why don't they teach breathing in schools? They should teach it. Maybe I will. Silence. So much silence.

I meet Dad's eyes and one eyebrow is raised in confusion. He is looking at me like I just told him that I bought him a pet alien for his birthday. Now, that isn't such a crazy thought after what I had experienced but I better not say that out loud. I hear Sankai giggle at my thought and the sound of her giggle melts me back into my heart just a little and I take another deep breath. I choose to see him in his greatness and project the lens of greatness all over him. With every moment of seeing him in his greatness he starts to shift. Almost like he is physically changing in reality, in my reality he is, but I don't know if anyone else is seeing what I am seeing. The more he changes, the more love I feel for him, the more I remember that I am responsible for how I perceive him. His posture gets taller, his eyes get brighter, his energy feels bigger and I feel closer to him.

Hmm that's better. I think to myself. There has been quite a silence now. I can feel Billie about to burst in the awkwardness. I know he wants to be a gentleman and let me do the speaking because this is meant to be my moment. Normally he would walk in and talk my dad's head off even when Dad wasn't listening. I am quite impressed with his restraint.

A part of me wants to keep the silence going just to see what happens when Billie actually bursts, but my heart knows that I already know how that one will go.

"We have had quite a journey today Dad. All I can tell you is it was a magical day and I do feel like a different person. No, not different, the same, just more of the same person. If that makes sense," I say.

"Well, kind of. I am glad you had fun. I can't say I can really understand what went on or even if I need to know. Billie, do you have anything you want to add? You've been standing there like a stunned mullet for the last two minutes. Normally you would be talking my ear off by now," Dad replies.

Why does he always do that? He will ask others the questions before me. I look at Billie. Billie looks at me awkwardly and takes a deep breath in.

"Well," he begins. "We have had a great day and we've had a lot of fun. A lot of laughs and ya know… those deep kinds of chats you have that just kind of… ummm… enlighten you?" He says with slight hesitation, to caution away from offending my dad by the remembrance of his late wife.

A moment of confusion washes over Billie's face. He doesn't know if he is feeling safe in this. Of course, he is safe but I can see that there is an element of feeling unsafe in his own words. His weight is shifting on his feet from side to side and he looks so awkward that I start to feel awkward. Is it possible that I am feeling what he is feeling? Ostara. Mate, don't you think anything is possible after the day you have had today? I think to myself. Yup brain you are right.

I take a deep breath and let out a sigh again but this time a long and lengthy sigh to ground myself a little more in the situation. This is ridiculous at how uncomfortable this is.

I decided to chime in. It's my turn to save Billie and I don't want to give Dad the space to pretend I am not here again. He does that when he is uncomfortable. I guess we are all human and all have our ways but I haven't learnt to accept this part of him. Yet. I hate it.

"We went to the magical paddock because we were doing some practicing for Billie. I won't go into too much detail because that is kind of private, but we ended up going deeper than we originally planned. I guess it all just unfolded like magic," I say.

I can feel my dad's body tighten at the word magic. I can feel the trigger in his heart. I feel myself respond to it. A response of instant guilt for speaking. Why do I do that? I have no reason to feel guilty in my logical mind but what I learnt today is that emotions aren't logical.

"Magic hey. Cooool. Cool. Cool. Cool," Dad responds with far too many cools. He gives himself away. He is trying to be cool about it but he is not cool about it at all.

I feel his pain. I feel a solid chunk of rock sitting in the left side of my chest and I somehow know it's not mine. I feel it so deeply and the moment I feel it, compassion takes over. How long has this been here for? How long has he felt such heaviness in his heart? Maybe always and I just haven't taken the time to notice it to this degree.

The compassion softens my shoulders, my breathing deepens, my chest opens and my eyes soften. It is like compassion has a mind of its own and starts moving my feet.

One foot in front of the other, yet floating. I feel like I am floating over to dad.

As I start floating he looks up from the ground with glazed eyes to meet mine. I feel his body tense even more as I get closer. As his body tenses the edges of my lips start to softly curl into a gentle smile of assurance. I stop right in front of him to meet him in an energetically intimate way, I hold a gaze with his eyes and I set the intention to see him in his greatness.

"You are great. You are the greatest of the great and I love you," I verbally vomit like I have no control over what I said. As soon as the words come out of my mouth, I can hear my mind get loud in disagreement with what I said but the compassion in my body feels very certain that the words are magic spells in this moment. I can feel the argument in my body between my fear and compassion like a tug of war but I hold my ground and keep holding the intention of seeing him in his greatness.

His face is blank but softer, his eyes look less glazed, and I can feel him arrive back into his body. Like his soul has just checked back in after a long holiday. And then. Within an instant of his soul coming through, my arms wrap around him and I squeeze tightly like I am giving a big bear a cuddle.

At first, I feel shock in his body and then he softens and his arms wrap around me. One hand on the back of my head and one on the back of my heart. I intentionally put my hands on the back of his heart to symbolically let him know that I am here to hold him. My fearful thoughts get really loud now.

'This is weird. It's too much. What if he rejects you tomorrow and there are no more hugs. What if he thinks you are crazy. We never hug; he might think we are on drugs. This is not safe. Love is not safe. Why do I have to be the one to do the fixing? What if I need fixing' It is all very loud. I hear

137

it playing like a record player around and around in my head and I simply listen like it's a movie desperate to have its show time.

What grounds me is hearing his heartbeat in his chest. It's slowing down with every beat and time feels like it has warped again. Time feels like it has slowed down to a point where all I can hear is his heartbeat. Baboom baboom baboom. Like a soothing remembrance of the time I spent in the womb being continuously connected to the sound of her heartbeat from the inside. In this moment I connect to the simple things that bring joy, the simplicity of the joy I feel in hearing my father's heartbeat. That he's alive, he is human and he is experiencing the whole spectrum of emotions like me, even if he is unaware of it.

I melt like butter even deeper into the embrace. As I melt deeper into the appreciation of the simple yet miraculous things about this moment, I take a deep breath to fully breathe it in and I sigh a peaceful sigh. As I melt, so does he. His breathing starts to become in sync with mine and he starts to gently rub my back.

In the background I can almost hear Billie's spirit applauding. He is lit up at seeing me and my father embrace so lovingly for the first time ever in Billie's eyes.

"I love you, Dad. I'm glad you are my dad." Again, words vomit out of my mouth without a second thought. So easefully and gracefully. I feel good about the words coming out of my mouth as I am sure they have come straight from my heart to his.

Instead, I feel his body tense again in rejection of my words. Our breathing comes out of sync and I can feel the disconnect slip into the embrace.

Fuck. Was I not meant to say that? Which part though?

And then I feel a single tear drop onto the top of my head as my head is tucked underneath his chin. I feel a sense of shame and again, somehow I feel as though it is not my shame.

It is his shame. Perhaps shame for the way he has fathered me or not fathered me. I don't dare ask as this is a progression in our relationship. Baby steps Ostara, baby steps.

I feel him starting to pull away and I feel sadness fall over my body. Time warped and it felt like forever but forever isn't long enough for my heart that has been craving this connection for so long yet denied it for myself in my own belief of being unworthy of it.

"Ah, you too kiddo," he whispers through a cracked voice.

He pulls away and pats me on my shoulder like a boss does to his colleague when they have done great work. He can't say it back meaningfully. Not yet.

"I am glad you had a great day. I've got some things I need to do in the shed but you two have fun hey," he says while he looks at me, looks at Billie and looks at the door all in one quick motion.

He pats me on the shoulder one last time and gives a slight smile to try and fool me into thinking he is happy and then he makes his way out the door.

Feeling a little confused but mostly satisfied with myself I turn to look at Billie who is now leaning up against the pillar of the door with his arms folded and legs crossed like he is right at home. He nods at me like he is giving me confirmation of a great job, almost like a judge of a singing show does when they are really enjoying the singer's performance.

"Well, I think you passed the test. Although it wasn't perfect, it was at the same time. Good job mate," he says as he is walking over.

"Thanks man." Is all I can get out before he wraps his arms around my head and squeezes my head into his chest in a big bear hug.

"There is still work to do, but it's progressing. What a day!"

"What a day alright! I still don't even know what happened," replies Billie.

"Yeah and we don't need to know. That's the point. But you need to go home and get some rest before tomorrow because tomorrow is the day that you do 'the do' with Melina," I say.

He winces in remembrance of what he needs to do but accepts the challenge like a warrior.

"Yup I am going to do 'the do'. I will leave you to it and see you tomorrow," he says and ruffles my hair like you would a pet dog as he sets back out the front door.

"Hey, Billie, do you think you will want these?" I point to his pile of clothes on the mantelpiece as he is still wearing some of my mother's clothes he found.

He bursts out laughing and so do I.

"Well now that would have been funny. I better get changed before I go. And THEN I will see you tomorrow," he says.

"Good idea. Thanks for being you, Billie. You bring me a lot of joy," I say with a smile.

He changed his clothes like lightening as he still had his school clothes on underneath my mother's dress.

"You too Star, you too," he says with an assuring smile and a wave as he walks out the door.

Chapter Nineteen

Ostara

I can feel the part of me that wants to be angry at my father and the part of me that wants to simply feel the love of him. I can feel this sense of a battle ground taking place in my body. I can feel all parts of me communicating to decide which one I want to make real, which one I want to choose to be at the forefront. As my hands are excavating and moving back and forwards from each other, pulling and pushing my energy in my hands, I can feel an internal aspect of me doing the exact same thing. I keep thinking to myself that I must be going crazy, this Ostara playing with her energy and feeling internal parts of herself is not the same Ostara from only this morning. It still baffles me. The whole thing seems like it will be a joke and someone will jump out from behind my door and yell out 'you got punked' any minute now. At least that is what I am telling myself.

My mind keeps recapping the day. Now I am comfy in my bed wrapped up by my blankets and following the new me who likes to explore things that are outside of this world as well as my internal world.

It is strange to think how disconnected myself and my dad have been for such a long time. Today was the first time since I was a child where I felt open to him, that I could deeply trust him to love me again and for myself to receive his love.

Although given a moment of feeling his heart again, he pulled away.

The part of me that feels rejected is angry, hurt, sad and resentful. The part of me that feels like there has been a progression is joyful, happy, loving and open. I can feel both parts having quite a time in my mind, battling it out for who is more powerful than the other, who deserves more of the attention and who is worthy enough to be chosen by me.

Yet one is not fighting, one is just holding presence and that is the part of me that is happy with the progression.

The other is throwing what you would call a tantrum but an internal tantrum, a bit like the one that I threw in the world of The Unconscious. The other is just holding space for the other to have its way with the emotions that come from the thoughts that are arising. What do I do here? I guess my only job is to witness it and then choose? I guess, but I am not certain.

"You simply wait, and let the expression run, let the thoughts run, the emotions have their space to express and then you choose to simply be in the middle yet focus on love. You choose which one you would love to be in and that's all you need to do," whispers Sankai.

She whispers so softly like she is conscious of disturbing my deep thoughts and introspection. Like she is in the room and she doesn't want to scare me. It is soothing. Her voice relaxes me.

Just choose. That's all I need to do.

"What would I love to be in the world? Which one would I like to be in the world? Well, that is obvious. One is very obviously aggressive and angry and the other is almost serene yet powerfully strong. I would love to choose the second one but isn't it important to have both expressed? Like I learnt in today's wild and wonderful experience of other worlds and parts of me?" I ask.

"Yes. But the very same act of listening, witnessing and being present with the part of you who is throwing a tantrum is the same as expressing it in the physical. You are always connected to everything through all time and space so if you are giving expression to this aspect of yourself in your mind through deep meditation then you are doing the same healing as you would in the physical. The physical is the last expression of magic," says Sankai.

'Huh?' An understanding yet baffled sound comes out of my mouth.

That makes sense. In the moment of understanding I get excited. So much can be done in the non-physical. Magic is real and THIS excites me!

So much of my own healing with Dad can be done here. Ahhhh I let out a sigh of relief. This makes life so much easier than I ever thought it to be.

"The healing can be in the non-physical but the action is what grounds the healing. The action is important, Ostara. Never forget that. Your actions can change everything in the tangible, and the tangible is important," says Sankai with a stern voice.

Action. Taking action. I think to myself. Such obviousness, so simple yet highly profound. Of course we need to take action. Derr. And that's what magic is, that's what makes it real. In the fairytales we are told that you can have a magic wand and simply wave it and poof something that we wish for suddenly appears. We are convinced that that is how magic works and to some degree it is but the only thing that is missing is the time. In fairytales the wand waves and it is instant but in life the wand is our choices and the puff of magic dust is our action and then it appears.

Woooahhhh even my own thoughts are blowing my mind and its limited comprehension.

Magic. Thoughts. Emotions. Actions. Result. Magic. Got it.

"One thing to watch out for Ostara is taking action when you are in an emotional charge. An emotional charge is when you feel an emotion so strongly that it almost feels like it could explode within yourself, at someone else or the world. This is when we come into the danger of acting from fear and not from love. You can choose from love at that moment but it takes practice. When we act from a charged emotion it is because we are letting that emotion rule us rather than choosing from what is true from our heart. There is no right or wrong way but what is true is that if more of the world chose from their heart and not the fear of a charged emotion the world would be a different place. Dark forces would have no power to thrive off, conflict would be inert and love would be the most chosen force of all. That is what heart-centred living can do. That is the power of choice that all living beings have. You have the power to choose every time but I urge you to be mindful that the choice comes from your heart and not your fear. You may fail this in your humanness but you will need to find forgiveness for yourself and others," Sankai says with her soothing tone.

I realise at this moment that I have mostly been taking action from my fear for the majority of my life. My mind clicks back through all of the emotional charges I have had in my life and I realise that most of my choices were because I was feeling abandoned by Dad and I wanted his attention or I stayed quiet because I believed he wouldn't see me anyway.

My mind quite literally feels like it is about to explode with these new realisations but in a good way, in a way where everything is coming together. The dots are starting to connect and a new path is paving in front of my mind's eye.

"When we follow our hearts there is always joy felt. Our heart will always lead us in the direction of what we need the most. Our heart will always guide us to feel a deeper sense of ourselves and the truth. The deeper we feel our pain, grief and sadness, the deeper we experience our joy and our pleasure. That is the gift of being human, that is the gift of feeling. As long as we keep our hearts open to every corner of human messiness then we'll always have a thread back to ecstasy and pleasure. It is the number one rule of this universe," Sankai continues as she responds to my thoughts.

"It's the cracks of the soul that allow more light to pour through to be seen and it's the light between those cracks that show us the way that allows us to be led from our hearts. As humans, we fear those cracks more than death. We fear to be seen as weak in our emotions yet what we perceive to be weakness is the golden ticket to a new world and a new way of living in love," she continues.

"This is the greatness that everyone so divinely desires. This is the greatness that we are moving towards," she whispers.

As she whispers these words I can feel my body sinking in a way that is settling. It is like I am settling deeper into myself with every word she speaks. Her words are like honey over my soul, soothing and gentle, sweet and delightful. In the moment of allowing the honey to set into my system an idea comes to me and the idea sends butterflies of nervous excitement through my heart.

I will teach this. I say to myself. I will start with myself and work outwards. I will plant seeds with my own actions and from there everything else will flourish and grow.

I am fully choosing to own this part of myself. I fully choose to be the vessel for this message in the world. This is my purpose. My message is my purpose. It only took me sixteen years to find it but I made it and what a gift it is to have found it. To have found myself.

As I sink deeper into the feeling of myself, of coming home to my essence I slowly start to slide down into bed from my seated position like I am melting.

My eyes are heavy and my heart is full, it has been a big day and I am ready to sleep and let it all sink in.

Tomorrow is a new day and who knows what it will bring.

"Tomorrow we are owning your true desires," whispers Sankai.

'Tomorrow we are owning your true desires' I repeat in my mind in agreement to her words. Whatever that entails I am ready, at least I think I am.

Chapter Twenty

Desires - Ostara's dream

I dance, I grind, I spin my body in all directions as I move to the muse of my body. Around me I see a forest of trees, flowers, honeybees, magic sparkles and small furry animals frolicking in the wilderness. I am the muse. A muse of desires. I am wearing red, gold and black and my clothes sparkle with diamantés. I feel like I am a different person to earth-bound Ostara.

I can feel this nature within me desiring to connect intimately with men and women, all humans and it doesn't matter who. Seduction pulses through me like a calling in of the essence of humans for me to ravish with my love. I run my fingers up and down my body as I dance in a way of honouring all of me. I feel animalistic, like I am on the prowl for my next meal.

As I dance to the juiciness of my body with my eyes closed, I feel the energy in my field radiate outwards like a beaker for all others to receive, to receive the pleasure of my own heart, of my own essence.

As I move and I dance as an embodied creature, my fierce energy calls upon different beings who are all walking towards me in a line. I continue to dance, to move, to stay in my body. I see men and women who are so beautifully desirable. I see an embodiment of wealth as one of these beings. Money personified with jewels, gold, a big smile and a heart that shines so brightly. I see a version of me who is healthy, fit, joyful and she wears clothes that scream pride. I see a child version of me who dances, sings, frolics towards me and dances around me in curiosity and adventure; she cares for nothing other than following her curious joy and innocence. There is a version of me who is older, she looks like the mother version of me, wise, grounded and soft yet equally as powerful, delightful and sensual. I see animals that I assume to be my spirit guides who are in animal form; one being a tiger, another a lion and another a wolf. They need not speak as their energy speaks to me loud and clear. Fierce and strong, wild and free, grounded and certain all while being fearless.

I scan my eyes throughout the forest seeing many creatures that all seem to be reflections of me. I feel connected to all of them in a way that words cannot explain, it is almost like I am living through them but a different lens. It feels as though they are here specially for me and I have arrived to give them the gift of my presence. The trees glow, and I can see veins of energy flowing through the trees from right down through the earth right to the tips of the leaves and outwards into the atmosphere. To the right are mountainous rocks, three very large stones that are red, pink and white and the stones shine so brightly they almost look like traffic lights and next to those traffic lights stands Billie.

I feel myself respond to the sight of him. It's a strange feeling to have such a strong reaction to Billie as I have never felt like that towards him before. I have only ever felt friend feelings, yet I love him so deeply and he brings me so much joy. What a gift this boy has been in my life and never have I felt these sexual sensations towards him before.

"What do you desire, Star?" he asks me. "Out of everyone here what gets a full yes from you? A full yes is when all of these stones light up. Oh and don't forget that you have mini stones in your body if you take a moment to look down," he continues.

As I hear him speak I am stopped in my tracks from my dancing yet my hips are still swaying slightly. I look at my body in the reflection of a puddle of water on the earth's floor and sure enough I can see three stones. One red in my womb, one pink in my heart and one white in the centre of my brain.

I look back at Billie and repeat to myself, "What do I truly desire".

I look around the forest at all of the beings here and go through them all. I first look at the wolf who feels like a symbol of going on adventures to bring back wisdom to the community and I ask myself 'Do I truly desire you' and all three stones get brighter. I guess that is a yes.

I notice out of the corner of my eye that there are flashes of a yellow colour and as I look in that direction I can see that the yellow is actually a sunflower with a face in the middle. I am not at all surprised by this, it feels fun, like this sunflower is also a reflection of me, plus I have always loved sunflowers. The sunflower has vines as arms and is almost fist pumping but in a gentle way. Wow this sunflower really is me. The sunflower starts to unload information onto me and I listen.

"Do you get a yes in all centres for the healthy version of you?"

All of the lights get brighter. Yes.

"Do you get a yes in all centres for the child version of you who is wild and free?"

All of the lights get brighter. Yes.

"Do you get a yes in all centres for the sexually embodied version of you?"

All of the lights get brighter. Yes.

We go through all of the beings that have come to me in this moment and I get a yes for all of them.

"All are a yes for you Ostara. Everything here is what you desire. It is time for you to own those desires," says the sunflower.

"Is there anything that I don't desire here?" I ask.

"Do you see that giant round container over there?" she replies.

Wow I didn't see that before. That just appeared out of nowhere. I am dreaming, vividly dreaming, so strange things are sure to happen here and I am open to it.

"Yup, I see it," I say.

"Well, this is a container for your life. A container that keeps you constrained to your identity. Ask yourself if you desire to be in this container?" she says.

I mentally ask myself the question and I notice that all lights in this rock go out and crack and my emotional reaction is disgust.

"Ew," I say with fire in my voice.

The sunflower giggles and waves her little vine arms around like she is dancing. She is so cute.

"See there are things in life that you don't desire. All you need to do is ask yourself and watch what happens to all three of your centres. Life is simple, fun, playful and all the joyful things. Following our full yes will always lead us in the direction of truth. I do have one more question for you... Do you desire Billie?"

All of the lights light up. Yes.

"Uhoh. No no no no. He is my friend. He is one of my ONLY friends. This dream isn't so fun anymore. I love him but I have never thought of him in that way before. Not that I think I have." I panic.

"Not that you have let yourself feel Star," says Billie.

Oh my god, dream Billie is inside my head.

"Yes, I am" He says as he suddenly teleports to be directly standing in front me of gently stroking my face.

I raise my eyes to meet his, suddenly feeling all of my centres firing with arousal. I can't fight it; the feeling is here and to my surprise it feels.... Good.

"See" he says. "Relax and follow what you feel".

His hands gently move down from my face and down onto my heart. My heart pulses with love and starts to expand as the love relaxes me even further. He holds my gaze with certainty in his eyes and an energy that speaks of a warrior heart.

My breath deepens as his hands start to run gently across my breasts and I can't help but let out a sigh of pleasure. My womb tingles and my ovaries swell with blood as arousal takes over me. It all feels so... natural. He feels so natural.

His hands come up to caress my neck as he pulls my face into his to meet my lips with the most passionate and heart-felt kiss. I melt. My hands start to wander around his body and suddenly we are laying on the ground, naked and wrapped around one another. I feel the warmth of his body against mine and the moist delight of his tongue in my mouth. My body is pulsing with life as it is connected with his. I feel the wetness of my pussy begging to be penetrated as my heart is on fire with passion.

"May I?" He asks so politely.

"Please" I respond.

Ever so gently he turns my head slightly to kiss my neck as he ever so carefully penetrates my very ready and engorged pussy. Pleasure ripples through my body as sounds escape my mouth. Our breath in sync and bodies moving as one. Every thrust brings a new sensation, a new opening in my body and his. Every thrust is a journey within itself then awakens more and more pleasure. His deep presence with me deepens mine and the pleasure raises rapidly. I feel a softening in my pussy as it expands to invite more of him in. Sounds continue to ripple out through my throat as the pleasure becomes too much. Orgasm explodes through my body and forces involuntary convulsions.

"Own your desires Ostara," whispers Billie.

ARRRGGGHHHH! I gasp and shock awake. Morning. It's morning and my heart is racing and my vagina is wet. What was that?! What a crazy dream. I seem to be spending a lot of time in the dreaming world. Even yesterday in the paddock felt like a crazy dream. What is reality? It is starting to feel like there is no separation between worlds, only lenses that we are perceiving through.

As I gently start to wake up my body after such a startle, I notice sensations in my body that weren't always there. Perhaps they could have always been there but I just never noticed. Regardless, it is something else that is new in my life. It seems to be a regular occurrence of new, strange and unexplainable things happening in my life. All these new changes, experiences and unfoldings of more of *me*. The sensation I feel in my body is a more intense tingle and I feel it right where my womb is, the same space that I saw the red light in my dream last night *and* where I invited Billie. Man, if things change so quickly in my physical body after dreams and celestial experiences I better be careful what I am dreaming about. What if I dream about the devil and I become him in the real world. Or what if I dream about having a child, does that mean I will wake up as a mother. What if Billie remembers that dream too. Oh hell. That would be a nightmare. Now I am starting to spiral. Oh no. Is that even possible? Is that something that will happen? Oh man. My brain is hurting, my head hurts. I have totally forgotten about the tingles in my womb that felt so nice, now it doesn't feel so nice anymore. Now it feels like fire burning in my pelvis. Oh boy. I feel anxious. I feel like I am losing it. Ok breathe, breathe, breathe, we aren't dying. What if we do die in our dreams, will I die then? Oh God. That's it, I am in a panic now. My breathing quickens, my heart starts to race and I feel sick to my stomach. "What is wrong with me?" I ask myself out loud. As tears start to pour from my defeated face. Sounds that I never thought would leave my mouth are leaving my mouth. I sound like a dying animal that is giving birth. The sounds are coming from the lowest pit of my stomach that feels like fire.

'Where are you in a time of need, Sankai,' I think very loudly and aggressively.

"I am always here Ostara but I only chime in when I need to," she replies.

'Is this NOT a time of need?! I feel like I am dying!" I reply aggressively again.

"Yes, but you are not dying. You are learning to trust in the unknown of your imagination, your intuition and your higher self that doesn't always make sense to a logical brain. Your higher self speaks through symbolism that you interpret. Just like your dreams. They are symbols to interpret that will create an energy shift but not to the point where you will completely shapeshift into an entirely different being. Human beings can't do that here in 3D but other beings can in other places. Just remember that Earth is different to other places and you need not worry about that," she responds in a calm manner.

Her words completely diffuse the fear that had arisen so quickly. I can now feel my body starting to relax and the remembrance that my own mind was just driving me crazy, not what is real. Although the uncomfortablity of having a sex dream about Billie is still there.

"Humans are such interesting creatures. They love to forget about magic because they can't understand it and much like yourself they will create terror for themselves thinking about all of the possibilities that could harm them rather than drinking in the here and now or even focusing on the magical possibilities for themselves. This is how humans became so disconnected from their own magic, by questioning everything they imagined *and* imagination is in fact intuition.

Humans have a love of torturing themselves like that. Not because it's what they want to do but because that's what the darkness has inflicted on them for eons. Just because the darkness is lurking, it doesn't mean you have to accept the invitation. You can say no in any given moment and yes to what feels more magic for you," she wisely expresses.

My body starts to melt a little deeper into myself again. Yes it is my brain and only my brain creating this fear. I am in the driver's seat. I am the one who is making the choices and feeding the cause of my heart. Yes, yes, yes.

"So just to clarify I am not going to end up with a baby after that sex dream? Or die if I die in my dreams? I mean, I know you just said no but can you say it again just because I am not ready to be a mother annnddd I have had some whacky dreams in the past and I don't want those to become reality. Hell no!" I say in my mind.

Sankai lets out a bellowing laugh.

"You are funny Ostara. No you won't become a mother if you dream about a child and you won't die if you die in your dreams. Your dreams are symbols of interpretation for you to gain insight into yourself and your life. For example, what did you learn from your dream last night?" Sankai asks.

"Well, I learned that I have desires that need to be owned and all these desires show up as different versions of me. I guess I need to work on those versions and create a relationship with each of them so I can own my desires. I also learned what sex is like, I hope sex in real life is like that, it was so passionate and… expansive. I still don't know why it was with Billie though. I say.

"Mhmmm imagine you do know, then what?" she says.

"Well… From what you have said I am guessing that he is just a symbol right? He is a symbol for maybe, er, um, the

155

passion and love that I am searching for so maybe that means that what I desire is to have more intimacy with my friends and maybe have more connection… Um. Yeah that's it," I say awkwardly as I am still unsure.

"Ostara, you do know that I have been with you for many lifetimes and know every single part of you. You cannot fool me in any way, my love, as much as you would probably like to. You have a desire to connect with Billie intimately, you just haven't allowed yourself to feel it yet as you have been too scared to end up alone," she says.

My stomach responds, my womb tingles again and my heart starts to race. Uh oh. The tingles are back I think to myself.

"That feeling that you are receiving now is a full body yes. The full body yes that you were learning all about in your dream last night. You know, the red, pink and white lights. They are symbols of your centres. When your centres respond with a tingle, a sensation or a knowing then it is a yes. If it is a full body yes then it is in your highest good to do that thing, otherwise it would be more detrimental to your health than anything else," she says with a stern feeling to her body.

The realisation is real right now. I think to myself.

"NOOOOOOO! He is my friend and one of my only friends. He likes Melina and we did the whole thing for him yesterday. I did that for him because he likes her and that's where his focus is, not with me and I did it for him because I love…" My thought trails off into a deep realisation. Fuck.

Because I love him. Oh no. I thought I always just loved him as a friend. He brings so much joy to my life and always has so I just assumed that it was because we are such good mates. How have I got this wrong my whole life? Or did it only just change recently? Or have I really not known myself for this long?

I become overwhelmed and start to cry again and this time I feel a pain in my heart for how disconnected I have been for so long. I feel disbelief that something so big could be so hidden for so long. Tears roll down my cheeks and as the cries come out of my mouth the pain in my chest that felt like a rock, starts to loosen. The more I cry the more I start to forgive myself, the more compassion I feel. I guess there are a lot of things I am learning about myself so why wouldn't this make sense too?

"Oh boy. What am I going to do about this one? What is the true action I am meant to take here?" I ask.

"Well, what is obvious to you?" asks Sankai.

"The obvious thing would be to talk to Billie about that, but it makes me want to vomit at the thought of doing that. I can't even imagine bringing myself to do that right now. He probably already thinks I am crazy after yesterday!" I say.

As the words escape my mouth I feel my phone buzz from under my pillow. Still feeling overwhelmed and unsure about everything that I am currently thinking and feeling I see a message from Billie. My heart skips a beat. Oh no. I don't need the extra anxiety about this Billie. I think to myself.

His message says *'Good morning sleepy head! Rise and shine, I am coming over in half an hour to walk to school with you and I just wanted to see if you needed anything after yesterday? Chocolate? A ball to bounce? Anything?'*

My heart flutters in my chest as I read the message. What a legend. He always has my back no matter what. Is it normal for all males to be this thoughtful? Or have I just found one of the best of the best?

As I sit in my moment of appreciation for Billie, I start to realise why I have a desire for him now. I realise it is things like this that make him so special. Apart from all the weirdness, the humour, the fun and the best mate vibes, he has such sensitive qualities that so many of the other boys at my school don't have, or do, but I just never see. Billie is so authentic in his expression and that's what I admire about him so much. I start to see why I could have a desire to connect with him intimately but I have never done that before.

I have never been with someone in that way before. I could have many times but I chickened out every time because I didn't feel like I was ready. Maybe I am ready now? Arggghh. This freaks me out as I am terrified of losing a friend.

First things first, do I want chocolate? Chocolate for breakfast? Hmm nope. But I do want it on the walk to school. Right, reply to Billie, Ostara, that's the first step, I think to myself.

I pick up my phone and reply with, 'Yes! Chocolate please. You are the best' and press send.

Maybe just dropping an extremely subtle flirt in there will send some signals of a conversation to come. Maybe that's a good idea. I will just work it in slowly over time.

And then I remember again.

OH. He is talking to Melina today. Today is the day that he tells the girl he has a crush on that he has a crush on her. I will just have to wait. This is extremely bad timing. Good one Ostara, great timing for such a big realisation. Why don't we just keep this one quiet for a while hey? I think to myself. Yes brain, I think that is probably a good idea for now. And no Sankai, I don't need your input right now. I think I have had enough.

I throw the covers off me and jump out of bed. 'It is time to get up and at em!' I give myself a small pep talk and get dressed. Even the smallest of tasks feel like they are a bit lengthier today.

I head out to the kitchen to prepare breakfast and I see Dad standing there with a cuppa in his hand looking out the window.

"Good morning, Dad," I say.

"Good morning honey," he says with a chirpiness to his voice. Honey? I have never heard him call me honey before. I almost felt scared with the weirdness of what he just called me. It feels weird but I kind of like it at the same time. The internal conflict is real. Before I even have another thought he wraps his arms around me and gives me a big comforting hug.

At first I feel my body go into a brief shock as my shoulders harden and then I soften. This is so nice. So, so nice.

A feeling I have been craving for such a long time that it doesn't take much to relax into it. I am more shocked about the honey thing but the hugs can stick around as long as they like.

"I had some crazy dreams last night which haven't happened for a long time. I haven't dreamt since you were a tiny unborn baby. I have always just slept but never remembered or experienced a dream again, but last night I did. I went on such a journey and I had so many realisations in that place. I mean, I can't fully explain all the details because it's not necessary but I can explain what I got out of it if you want to hear?" He beams. "Oh and I made you some toast," he continued.

My heart flutters in excitement. Who? How? What has happened to my dad? He looks and feels like a totally different person but I am not at all complaining.

"Wow, thank you. And YES! Yes, tell me all of it. I want to hear it. We have twenty-five minutes until Billie gets here so take that time to share," I say.

He places toast with peanut butter and banana in front of me and I feel my heart flutter again at the thought of eating peanut butter and banana on toast that my dad made for me. What a time to be alive, I think to myself. Today is a good day.

"So," Dad begins. He says it with such energy that I am dying to hear what he has to say. Is he experiencing the same magic that I have been experiencing? Maybe it's a ripple effect kind of thing.

"I was in a really dark place, like a cave but the cave didn't have edges. It was like it was a never-ending dark space. Perhaps you could call it hell or something but it didn't have the burning fire that most of the biblical stories tell you it has. While I was there it felt totally empty. Like there was so much potential but no potential at the same time. It was totally neutral. I don't think I have ever experienced anything like it in my waking or dreaming life for that matter, even when I dreamt in the past. So I was standing there and I don't know why I was standing there. I mean, dreams are like that. A bit wild, a bit weird and incomprehensible at the best of times. Anyway, I saw this dark figure come in and it was ugly, like demonic. I felt intimidated but I didn't feel scared. Like I had seen this figure before. Long story short. It cast some sort of spell on me and I couldn't help but turn into an absolute caveman. I was expressing myself like a wild man. A man who is… uncivilised. I had no control over it. I was punching the ground, screaming, crying, laughing, thrusting, throwing a tantrum, shaking, it was all VERY weird. Everything you could think of. Whatever kind of movements you could think of I was doing it. And then. This is the interesting part. I saw your mother. After some time of being a wild caveman in expression I saw her standing next to this demonic being like they were buddies. She was as beautiful as she always was, like a goddess with such divine presence. Normally I try not to think about your mother because there is so much pain there."

Tears start to well up in his eyes and quickly fall down his cheeks. I have never in my entire life witnessed my dad cry or express anything. I am so shocked my mouth falls open mid chew on my toast and I can't help but stare.

"But here I felt excited to see her like she was real. Like she had never left. I, for the first time in a very, very long time felt…" he pauses.

"Love and happiness. I felt happy. Happy to see her. Happy to think of her. Happy to be existing. And then it was like she just whipped me in the face with harsh truth. She said 'My love, this is NOT ok. You have not allowed yourself to feel since I chose to leave this Earth and in doing so you are choosing not to take part in this world. It is better to die after a full life than choosing death while living. Feeling is what makes you alive and our daughter needs you. Wake up. Wake up to yourself. Wake up to this life and wake up to what is in front of you. Let yourself feel it all, the good and the bad and you will have the power to live in love again'. Her words cut through me, Star. It was like she was saying it to me in real life. It was so vivid. I don't know what had changed to make this dream so damn real but it was so real that I can't ignore it. Other stuff happened but that is the main gist of what the message was," he says.

Tears are still falling from his cheeks and they increase as I see him preparing for more words.

"I am sorry if I haven't been the father you wanted or needed, Star. I am sorry that I haven't been present all these years. I am not perfect but I promise that I will work on it from now on. This was such a profound experience for me that it has changed something in me. I don't know how it will be different from here but I know there will be a difference. I am willing to do better, be better, talk more, be more. Because in all realness, the caveman expression gave me so much relief in my dreams. It felt good to go wild. I am not going to say that I will do that because that seems too much in 'normal' life but I am choosing to wake up now to what I have, and that means waking up to you as my daughter. I am sorry, Star, for all the pain I have caused you."

He really starts to blubber now as the guilt overcomes him. I attempt to chew the toast that is still sitting in a ball in my mouth so I can speak, but the peanut butter is like cement so all I can do is hold his hand and put my other hand on his shoulder. The moment I touch him he takes a deep breath and raises his head to look me in the eye like a wounded warrior.

I give him a hearty and grounded smile while I am chewing the last piece of my buttery toast. I guess I am not meant to be saying anything at the moment.

"Things will be different, I will be different and I want you to know how much I love you Ostara, and always have. Even if I seemed like I didn't show it," he says.

I finally swallow the sticky toast.

"I know Dad. I know." I pause for a moment to wait for more words to come. "We all have challenges in our life. We all have pain and deal with it differently. You are my Dad and I love you as you are. I am looking forward to seeing this new you and however this new you is, I promise to love that version of you too," I say with assuredness in my voice.

He nods his head at me with a slight smile as he acknowledges what I have said. His eyes dart to the left and he wipes his eyes and sniffs swiftly.

"Hey Billie," he says as he tries to hide his 'unmanly' tears.

My heart skips a beat and I turn around to look at the door and sure enough there he is, standing there looking slightly surprised and awkward.

"Sorry I didn't mean to interrupt. I can wait outside," says Billie.

"No, no, we're finished here. Star is late for school anyway thanks to me, so you better be off. I've packed your lunch in your backpack so you'll be ready to go," Dad says, standing to kiss me on the head.

I gulp as I know what is next. There is no escaping my conversation with Billie but after my hearty connection with Dad, my heart feels softer. It all feels less scary yet terrifying all at the same time.

Chapter Twenty-One

The truth will set you free

My heart is pounding in my ears, it feels like it might pop into my throat. I can, quite literally, feel my heart beating in my throat and it is so uncomfortable. I am looking at Billie as I walk beside him. I can see his mouth moving as he is verbal vomiting a story at me and so beautiful as he does it. I can see his lips moving but nothing is computing in my brain as I am so focused on what I need to say yet not saying.

I don't think I can do this. I don't think I can say the words. The words make me feel like I want to vomit. I do want to vomit. Oh God. What if he rejects me and never wants to be my friend again then I will be alone forever, I will die alone. Oh God. What if he laughs at me and makes fun of me. What if he doesn't believe me and thinks I am joking, how will I get out of that one? Oh God. Such noisy thoughts. So much noise. It's so goddamn loud!

I am staring at the ground now, trying to focus on the steps in front of me. I wonder if he has noticed anything weird about me yet. Oh please don't. Please don't ask me because then I will have to speak it.

The vomit is swirling around in my stomach and it could come up at any moment. Ok, Ostara, remember your breath… remember all that you have learned in the last forty-eight hours. Yup, there is a lot of information this crazy brain of mine is learning but if all else fails remember your breath.

Breathe. Breathe. Breathe. I inhale deeply and my belly and chest expand. They expand so much that I feel like it is not just me that is actually breathing. Even the space around me is breathing. I exhale a long, lengthy breath.

Phaorr. That's a bit better. I feel myself come back down to earth again, like my feet have just landed back here for the first time since seeing Billie again.

"Are you ok?" I hear Billie say. I snap back into fear again. Well that peaceful state was short-lived. The vomit sensation comes back again and I take another deep breath as my heart races in my throat again.

"Errrmm… Yeah. I am ok. I mean it has been a big forty-eight hours, ya know. I am still landing back here and…"

"Has it ever!" Billie interrupts. "It has been such a time for you Ostara! I mean I have been here with you but you've been on more of a journey than me. A journey that I still don't really understand and I am hoping that one day I will. Even I am starting to think I am going a bit mad," he continues.

I feel a sense of relief that he interrupted me so I don't have to speak again. Anything to get out of this conversation. Yet I know deep down it needs to happen. It is like there is an anchor on my heart and that is what is keeping me going through all of this fear and discomfort.

"I guess if I am going mad then I am sure you are going mad too. How are you feeling after everything yesterday? Any other news you have to tell me after I left?" he asks.

Amazing. I think to myself. For the last ten minutes I hadn't heard a single word he had said, or replied to any of it and he just talked away to me and didn't notice a thing. Such innocence. It fascinates me. It is genius really. I don't know anyone else who can do that. He is a special kind of human.

"Well… ermm. Yeah. There were a few more things. A few more… Ermm… lessons or messages that I learned very loud and clear. I am just processing them and umm, yeah, I'm a little or a lot nervous about them," I say and smile at him awkwardly, sideways without looking at him in the eye. If I look him in the eye I might crack. I feel like I am about to pop like a balloon.

"Hmm well… I'd like to hear it if you are ready to speak about it? Can you speak about it or is it one of those things that are hard to explain like The Unconscious place you experienced yesterday that I am still trying to wrap my own head around?" he asks.

"Well. It's like one of those things. It's more so that I learned a big thing about myself," I say.

I feel the tension in my stomach get tighter as I look up at him. Everything feels like it is in slow motion again and I can see his lips moving, his hands moving to the rhythm of his words that he is vomiting out of his mouth. There is a sense of peace and calm here, even though the moment feels like such a short moment. It feels calm. Like there is nothing to worry about and it will all be fine regardless of what happens or doesn't happen.

"The truth will set you free, Ostara." I hear Sankai whisper in my mind.

The truth will set you free. The truth will set you free. The truth will set you free. The words echo in my mind and I have absolutely no idea what Billie is speaking about. Nothing at all and that doesn't bother me because I feel my will power turn on. I feel a warmth inside of my core right above my belly button and as it turns on, I feel my posture straighten, my vision become clearer, my breathing becomes deeper and my hearing turns on again.

"I mean it's all a bit of a dream…" I hear Billie say as my hearing switches on and then it happens.

"Billie, I need to tell you something right now," I say as I grab his arm to stop him in his tracks and face me. I feel ill again but this time it feels more bearable.

"I am freaking out about speaking these words but I have to. I wish I didn't have to but I do and I know that I do because I wouldn't have received true information to not speak it. I mean I can, but I can't because I would burst like I am right now. It has been a huge forty-eight hours and I am still working out whether or not I have gone mad. I am totally questioning my sanity but at the same time I have never felt more me than I do right now. I have never felt more connected to myself AND to my mother. I… I…ummm," I fumble.

Ok breathe, Ostara. I think to myself.

"So… Last night… another one of those crazy things happened to me in my dreams. I can explain the full details later after I just get out what I need to say. I had a crazy thing happen and… Well… I realised that… That I… Ummm… I think I have more feelings for you than just friends. I never in a million years thought I would say that because you are my best friend. The only great friend I have ever had and I have been so blind to it for all of these years but it makes sense, it makes sense. You get me. You know me better than anyone. You have been there for me through everything in life. You can make me laugh like no one else can. You have such a kind heart and you have always loved me even in the craziest of times in my life like last night. You have never judged me, always stuck up for me and supported me in every way. I have always just thought of you as a friend and I have honestly never opened myself up to the thought of anything else but last night something changed and I can see the truth in it, even if it doesn't happen in reality, I can see it and I had to tell you. I have never thought I was worthy of love in the first place for all this time. I never thought that anyone could ever love… Me… plain old Ostara, who was always a little strange in the world, a recluse of some sort. Yet, you have always been there and I just… I just love you, Billie. I love you so much as a friend and as someone who I am finally admitting has all the characteristics that I would love to be with because you are someone I trust my life with.

"I know it might sound crazy and I have been freaking out about this but I need to say it because I tell you everything so of course I need to tell you this. You don't have to respond straight away. I know it might be a big shock, it is to me too, but I just need to say it. There is something more here Billie. I don't know where that something more will lead or what it entails but I just know there is something to explore, it is ok if it doesn't happen but I just had to say it, I just had to have radical honesty with you." I take a deep breath and finally look him in the eye.

His eyes are wide open like a stunned mullet and his mouth has fallen open. I don't think he breathed at all in the last minute or so. It looks like someone has pressed pause on him. I almost want to wave my hands over his face to see if anyone is home.

Now I feel ill again. It's out there now and I can't take it back. The moments waiting for him to speak feel like an eternity.

He starts to make noises with his mouth like words are trying to come out but nothing is happening.

"Breathe, Billie" I blurted out as the tension was killing me.

I see him take a breath and another and watch him slowly come back to earth again.

"I… Um… I don't know what to say, Ostara. This is a total shock. I feel like you have just punched me in the face and I am trying to find my glasses to see again. I mean… WHAT? Where did this come from? Only yesterday we were talking about Melina and today is meant to be the day and now you throw this on me? I was already nervous enough about Melina. And now… and now you've thrown this at me. I know you had a lot happen in the last day and you've been through a lot so maybe you are just confused, I don't know. I sure as hell am. I feel confused. In fact, I feel a bit angry. I feel angry that all of this is happening and I feel like I don't have any control over it. I really can't deal with this right now. I don't know how to deal with this," he says.

He shakes his head and refuses to look me in the eye totally aloof from the situation.

"I just… I just need to go. I need to go to school and get on with my day. I am sorry but I want to go by myself. Just leave me alone for a while please," he blurts out with frustration in his voice. He kicks the gravel underneath his feet and huffs as he starts to walk off.

"Billie!" I yell.

"Please just leave me be, Ostara," he yells back without turning around.

My heart aches and feels heavy in my chest. I feel a well of emotions come over me. I am in total disbelief. Billie and I have never had a fight, or disagreement, or anything of the sort. Have I just ruined my life?

My heart contracts and the pain takes over.

Chapter Twenty- Two

The Reckoning

My heart is screaming on the inside. In my imagination I can hear a little girl crying in my heart. I hear her crying but I am totally numb as my eyes watch Billie walk over the horizon. My feet are planted on the ground underneath me and have not moved at all since he walked away. My heart is pounding in my ears like I have earmuffs that are holding in the sound. My body feels like a speaker throbbing with pain that is trying to force its way out but the music is distorted. The music of my soul is no longer a beautiful heart song but a raging death metal concert with fighting mosh pitters full of aggression.

Breathe, breathe, breathe, Ostara.

I close my eyes to focus on my breathing and I listen. Inhale. Exhale. Exhale with sound. Inhale. Sigh. Inhale. Growl. Inhale. Wail. Inhale. Inhale. Wail. Inhale. Sound. Inhale. Let go. Inhale. Sound.

The more I let go, the more I let the sound out of my mouth, the more me I feel, the more in my body I become. There is still an aching pain in my chest but it is no longer feeling unbearable. I open my eyes and there is no more Billie. He has gone over the horizon and it is now just me.

Just me. All alone with this ache in my chest. Feeling as though no one in the world cares about me, even though I know they do but it doesn't feel like it at this moment.

This feeling feels awfully familiar. It is how I have felt with Dad all these years. I have felt like a floating cloud going unrecognised or cared about, only to now, sixteen years later feel a shift in him.

This does feel awfully familiar. Like I am in a repeating pattern of my relationship with Dad but with Billie. If I can shift my relationship with my Dad then I can shift my relationship with Billie too. Maybe he won't want to talk to me ever again and I will be alone forever but maybe I do have the power to change it?

I may be going crazy and it might be a total waste of my time but something needs to happen right now and I know that I can't stay like this.

"Simply listen, Ostara. Listen to what the child in your heart is saying. Just like you did in the Astral world of your heart, listen. Awareness is everything. Gain awareness, focus on the vision and take action towards the vision. First, listen and receive yourself," I hear Sankai transmit to me through my own thoughts. It could totally be my thoughts that are making all of her words up, yet I know it is her as she sounds different in my mind.

Maybe we are crazy Ostara or maybe we are now a spiritual gangster. I think mockingly to myself.

"I think, spiritual gangster," Sankai says with a chuckle in her voice.

Her words bring me a sense of grounded-ness. Like my willpower becomes switched on again as I feel the fire inside of my rage. My fire knows my fucking worth. My fire knows it is ok to feel this pain and there is no way to hide from it. This fire in me is ready and willing to dive into the wildness of my pain, be consumed and to rise like a phoenix from the grave.

"Bring it fucking on," I whisper under my breath while I still stare at the horizon.

I let out a cry like I am about to enter a battle. I growl, I howl, I jump up and down, stomp my feet on the ground and I let the fire rip through the pit of my stomach and out through my mouth. The animal in me takes over and the savage emerges from the depths of me to be expressed. The savage who gives no fucks about who gets in her way. The savage that has no fear in any battle. The savage who is willing to take on the pain to serve her cause.

I am here letting the savage express. My body moving like an animal and sounds escaping my throat that feel like they could not possibly be coming from little old Ostara. And then I feel a pop of the energy around me and the world within me The fire penetrates my heart and grief comes over me. The child in my heart now takes over, her desire to be held calls me.

Only, I am the child. I wrap my arms around myself to hold myself.

"I have got you and I am not going anywhere," I whisper to myself like I am re-parenting myself and as I sink into holding myself, the tears pour from my eyes.

As the tears fall and the sobs leave my throat, the pain in my chest starts to loosen and my breathing deepens.

"I feel invisible," she says.

"I know little one, but you are not because I see you," I reply.

She smiles a slight smile and nods.

As my heart receives my words, she expands and my entire being expands with it. Like a melting into myself as a new clarity has formed.

I feel energy pour from somewhere out of the space around me and down into my feet. In my imagination it feels like God is watering me like a pot plant, washing away all of the pain and heaviness from my body and bringing lightness back into me.

I immediately feel connected to everything around me again and the pain from my body no longer feels like pain, only a distant memory of what I thought my reality was. Only an illusion. I feel connected to essence and grounded in my power again. I feel like a whole new me has simply entered my body and the old Ostara has been laid to rest. I feel the child version of me, the scared child who is trapped in her mind of insanity as she makes everything about herself and what it is to be in the world. I feel the child version of me who has been so desperate all of her life to prove the worthiness of her humanness slowly and seductively dying. I feel her growing up and out of my skin as I shed. It has only been two days and I feel as though layers have fallen from my being and new layers have taken their place.

I feel the layers of me that want to tear the world to the ground for my purpose. The part of me that will never give up in the fight for service in the world. I feel her breathing through me penetrating every step. I feel a warrior spirit dancing through me.

I feel the layers of me that are devoted to love; in the messiness of love, the pain of it, the joy of it, the pleasure of it and the truth of it. I feel the dedication to creating from the centre of my heart.

I feel the layers of me that are badass. The layers of me that are more mother-like than maiden. A mother who is only here to provide care for the children of the future and I feel the father in me who is devoted to the feminine in me. Who

173

is devoted to my mission and purpose that has unwavering strength for all adversity that arises and will arise.

Only two days and so much has moved. It makes me question how I am still standing.

I never thought it would feel so good to be so wild and so free in the expression of my body. I never thought it would feel so unashamedly true in every way that my emotions move through me. Why is this not taught in schools? I ask myself. It should be.

And then I remember.

"This is my purpose!" I say out loud.

I remembered what Sankai has led me to discover within myself; that I will teach this.

"Teaching this work is my destiny! This is my greatness. That's how I am still standing, because it gives me energy. Damn why would I choose a destiny so challenging?" I ask out loud.

"Because life would be boring without the challenges. Life is about overcoming the might of the dragons and discovering the power of each princess in every battle. You are the dragon slayer, Ostara. The dragon slayer that's also friends with them too," says Sankai.

"I am the dragon slayer. I feel as though I have slayed about twenty dragons in the last two days and created one. I'm a badass!" I say.

But what to do about Billie. I ask myself.

"There is nothing you need to do. You have done all you need to do. It is up to him now how he deals with it. The challenge of speaking the truth was your dragon, Ostara, the transformation of darkness into light. The challenge was doing the most loving thing for yourself which was also one of the hardest things to do. You have well and truly passed the test," Sankai says.

"The test?" I ask with slight frustration. "Was all of this testing for some sort of celestial fairytale story? If that is the case then that is bullshit because I didn't even have a choice in the matter. I would like to at least have a choice!" I say with fire in my voice.

"You *always* have a choice, Ostara. Always. You have had soul contracts that you signed as a celestial being before you decided to come into Earth as a human. You signed contracts to go through everything you have gone through and your only job is to live them and come home to remembering more of yourself. And that is exactly what you have done. You have done an incredible job at staying grounded in all of this. You should be proud of yourself," Sankai says with warmth in her voice.

The warmth of her voice feels like honey pouring over my skin. Soothing and softening the fiery frustration I feel. Her voice pours over my body and meets my heart and I instantly come home.

Home is where the heart is as they say and now I get it.

There is no way I am going to school. There is no part of me that wants that for myself. Not at this moment.

What would I love right now? I ask myself as I am so deeply connected to the sweetness of honey in my heart.

'Close my eyes and sing my heart song' is what I hear in my mind as I ask the question.

"And sing my heart song is what we will do, little treasure," I speak out loud to myself.

I start to hum and sway my body and I feel the vibration through my chest. I feel the vibration moving the parts of me that are not of the physical human body. I feel energy moving and vibration swirling.

With my eyes closed and vibration moving me, my imagination goes wild and opens like a crevice of a curtain in the wind.

Through the curtain I see a blue and gold alien-like being with golden eyes, a white robe and white and golden hair. He is beautiful, and somehow I know he is a he even though he could be a woman too. His eyes look like a golden star system swirling around and his energy is so inviting. He puts his hand through the curtain as if to invite me through with his guidance. I pause for a moment in fear but the fear only lasts for a second.

"Come with me, I have a gift for you. Many gifts. You are safe and I wish to be in your presence," he says.

'Yup you are trippin' again,' I think to myself.

Feeling somewhat like royalty I take his hand. What could possibly go wrong, I think and my feet are no longer on the earth.

Epilogue

The Beginning

I come to consciousness again without any sense of time or understanding of how I got to where I got to, like I entered some sort of worm hole but have no memory of the journey. Total amnesia.

I have no sense of my body, yet I still feel a connection to it, like I know that it is safe but I am not in it. It is the strangest of feelings, yet so comforting. It feels like home, like I have been here many times before. There is no fear here. Nothing at all. And fear is an emotion that I so often feel.

I simply feel like a floating bubble, unable to see my body. In front of me is this blue and gold being who pulled me into this space and I am still in awe of his beauty. He is floating, yet he looks like he is standing on something tangible but it's not. It is simply energy he is standing on. My mind trips out for a moment and again questions my sanity and whether it is real but the thought fades quickly as the gratitude of this experience enters my feeling body.

"It is real; magic one. Magic is real and I am simply an aspect of the magic realm that is not of the earthy sort. I am of the Pleiadian sort. This dimension is the fifth dimension, you are of the third. You have tangibility about you whereas I/We here are simply energy that have not manifested into the tangible so many know nothing about us. You however, we have been watching closely for quite some time now. The moment your mother birthed you into Earth we have been watching you, waiting for the moment of truth to open, for your readiness to give us permission to ask for your help. And my name is Zodak," he concludes.

"*My* help? This doesn't make any sense. When you just said I am of the third dimension, that means I am not of this dimension, so how can I help you? I don't know anything about this place?" I ask.

"Ahhh, that's where you are wrong my dear. You have chosen this path for yourself and we equally chose you for the job. You see there are things you need to know and there are more gifts for you to receive. The safety of the Logos depends on your willingness to fulfill your purpose. Sankai has been your guide for many, many lifetimes and she has done well to guide you this far. She will continue to guide you when you return home to the earthly realm, but for now, there is work to be done here and if you let me, I will show you everything in one fine swoop. I will show you everything you have forgotten about this world. I will show you everything as to why you are the one we have been waiting for and I will show you why we need you. The sacred scrolls of the fifth will be delivered to you never to be forgotten again. Oh, and I will give you your light weapons, you will need those," he says.

Light weapons. Sacred scrolls of the fifth? Right. This seems like some trippy movie that I have actively made up in my mind. I expect myself to wake up at any moment and this is all a dream. But still, I don't feel any fear here, just a sense of home.

My focus is on Zodak and I ponder his words.

"Well, I have come this far, there is no point in going back. I don't even think I can go back after everything I have experienced in the last few days. I have no idea what is ahead of me and there is uncertainty in that, but if I go back I will be forever wondering what this journey might have entailed. A part of me wants to go back and I can feel the pull of saying no, but there is something deep inside my heart that is keeping me here and I am not sure what that is. I guess I will find out. Can you tell me one thing before we go any further?" I ask.

"Potentially," Zodak replies.

Uncertainty washes over me again. "Has my mother got anything to do with this journey? Did she sign these contracts for me to be the person you want me to be?" I ask with slight desperation in my voice.

Zodak smiles at me with a warm smile. Nothing. Nothing comes out of his mouth. Yet his smile somehow feels like confirmation of truth in what I have said. He speaks nothing yet his body speaks a thousand words.

"It is time to know everything, dear magic one. It is time to meet your destiny," he says as he floats over to me with such grace and beauty. He places his shiny gold and blue palm on my forehead and I am sucked back into yet another portal.

To be continued in book two...

About the Author

Paige Mirco's journey started deep in the forests of the south west of Western Australia on an organic permaculture farm with her family.

Her love for channelling, healing, astral projection, magic and spiritual connection was inspired by her father who spent a large part of Paige's life teaching her the knowledge he knew. Later in life Paige took it upon herself to learn more and dedicate her life to being a truth seeker. She spent years studying many different healing modalities and researched heavily into esoteric nature. Paige later went on to become a teacher, facilitator and mentor in the field of self-development and healing. She has an unwavering devotion to guiding others in remembering their heart as their compass which is what she believes will lead them and the world to a life of love, freedom and unity.

One of Paige's greatest loves is teaching wonderful students in an online course called Synchronise Me and working with individuals in a 1:1 capacity to stretch the magic of the heart as far and as wide as possible. Paige has helped hundreds of people reconnect with the magic in their heart and live a life beyond their limitations.

She is a devoted writer in many forms such as story, poetry, blogs, newsletter, social media and more, and she will continue to write as this is a powerful way to get her message out into the world. She will continue to do so until her heart tells her to stop (if that ever happens).

Paige also has a passion for fitness, natural health and organic farming and lives this lifestyle with her beloved partner in the Sunshine Coast of Queensland Australia.

To find out more about Paige's work in the world visit: https://www.thejoycatalyst.com.au/

Printed in Australia
Ingram Content Group Australia Pty Ltd
AUHW021016250624
396163AU00001B/1

9 781763 603004